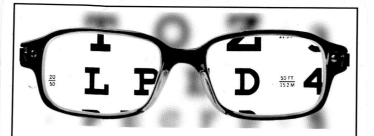

If you are only able to read large print, you may qualify for Wolfner Library services which include free access by mail to:

- Over 350,000 titles in audio and other formats
- Use of audio playback devices
- DVDs with descriptive narration
- Over 70 audio magazines

Wolfner Talking Book and Braille Library

Email: Wolfner@sos.mo.gov
Toll free: 800-392-2614 (in Missouri)
Phone: 573-751-8720

OUTLAW VALLEY

Max Brand

writing as
Evan Evans

OUTLAW VALLEY

G.K.HALL &CO.
Boston, Massachusetts
1992

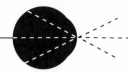

**This Large Print Book carries the
Seal of Approval of N.A.V.H.**

Published in Large Print by arrangement with
the Brandt & Brandt Literary Agency and the
estate of Frederick Faust.

G.K. Hall Large Print Book Series.

Printed on acid free paper in the United States of
America.

Set in 16. pt. Plantin.

Library of Congress Cataloging-in-Publication Data

Brand, Max, 1892–1944.
　　Outlaw valley / Max Brand writing as Evan Evans.
　　　　p.　　cm. — (G.K. Hall large print book series)
　　(Nightingale series)
　　　　ISBN 0-8161-5601-8
　　　　1. Large type books.　　I. Title.　　II. Series.
　　[PS3511.A870843　1992]
　　813′.52—dc20
　　　　　　　　　　　　　　　　　　　　　　　92-18522

1

AT FIRST HE had no name; and that was not odd, seeing that when he appeared in the village he neither spoke nor appeared to possess hearing, nor bore a sign that would tell people how to call him. He was dressed in a good gray suit, such as businessmen the world over are apt to wear. He had in his hand a slender walking stick, and in his pocket there was a wallet of dark, time-polished pigskin which, when opened, gave out only a small handful of dollar bills.

Everything about this man was neat and precise. He was well barbered and well tailored. There was no outdoor tan on his skin, but it was pink-tinted and clear—the skin of an athlete, as if he were one of those thousands who keep fit in city gymnasiums, squash courts, or swimming tanks. He had smooth, regular features; his hair was a dark, glossy brown; his step was light and swinging; indeed there was little about him to suggest age. One might have picked him to win a tennis match or come in well in front in a golf match. And yet everyone in the town who saw him judged him to be fifty at the least.

Even on that first day he attracted a good deal of attention. The town of Lister is so small that if a strange dog barks within its precincts every boy and every housewife notes the new noise; and of course the appearance of this deaf mute excited everyone to the utmost. That excitement grew when the list of his purchases was made known.

From his appearance, he would have been set down as a rich man on a Western vacation, quite careless of price, but his actions were out of harmony with that idea. He took five dollars in his hand and went from one new gun to another in the rack at Bowen's General Merchandise Store, until Bowen himself, in a temper, wrote down on a piece of paper in large letters: "Five dollars won't buy so much as the trigger of one of these guns!"

The stranger seemed shocked to hear this, and young Sandy Larkin suddenly remembered the Winchester .45 which hung on the wall of his father's room. Once it had blown large holes through Indians; but now it was good only to be talked about, and it was coated inside and out with rust. Sandy beckoned the stranger after him and led the way to his house. The latter took down the gun, examined it for an hour with the most painful attention, and then gave his five dollars for the relic.

When they passed out through the yard of Sandy's house, he was attracted by an axhead which he kicked up out of the dust beside the chopping block. This he examined with almost as much care as he had given to the rifle. It was an old pattern, made of the stoutest of German steel when German steel was the best in the world, but it had a fat-bellied bevel and it was heavy and clumsy to a degree. It seemed to suit the stranger, however. He offered twenty-five cents for it and got it for thirty. From Sandy, also, he secured an old adze hanging at the side of the woodshed, for a dollar and a quarter. The day of the adze was gone in the town of Lister.

Returning to Bowen's General Merchandise Store, he now looked over the knives and bought the two best blades in the collection, as Bowen declared afterwards. They were long in stock, prohibitively priced, and the stranger picked them out

3

quickly enough from the long case where the hunting knives were displayed.

"He's been in the steel business," said Bowen afterwards with much confidence. "Otherwise how could he of known?"

After this, a quantity of powder and a roll of lead was bought, a tarpaulin, a blanket, some salt, and a little flour. The stranger made a pack clumsily enough, walked a mile out of the town, and then returned.

He took what appeared to be his last coin from his pocket. It was a twenty-five-cent piece, and when he pointed to a coil of strong rope, Bowen cut off a dollar's worth and gave it to the singular adventurer.

After that, he marched away with a long, strong step, and he was last seen headed for the highest mountains.

For two months Lister buzzed about him.

It was Sandy Larkin who brought down the first authoritative word about him. Sandy, on a hunting trip, had become widely separated from his companions on the gulley-riven side of Mount Shannon, and there, in a narrow little valley, he came on a newly built cabin whose logs bore the marks of fresh chippings. In front of it he found a stone oven, most crudely built.

When he opened the door, he found that inside there was nothing but a homemade chair, a rude table, and a pile of pine boughs for a bed in one corner. Also, around the walls, were a number of coyote, lynx, and wolf skins drying on stretchers.

Sandy found a quarter of venison, and, being very hungry, he helped himself to it in true mountain style, and built a fire in the stone oven to cook it. In the midst of this cookery, the owner returned, and Sandy recognized him at once as the deaf mute who had astonished Lister two months before. He was greatly altered, for now he was brown, very thin, and his gray suit had been torn to tatters which were roughly mended with sinews. His shoes had given out, and on his feet were shapeless moccasins of ridiculous manufacture.

He appeared glad to see Sandy, and with a smile and a wave of the hand seemed to offer the boy all the hospitality which the cabin afforded. Then he put down his rifle and went inside to get salt.

While he was gone, Sandy looked at the old gun. It was well cleaned and oiled, and Sandy learned that the stranger had fitted it with handmade ammunition. He saw many other details of the curious housekeeping of this man and returned to Lister full of what he had seen. Before he left, he had written on the back of an envelope: "You'd better get out of here before the snows begin. It will be terrible cold here!"

But the stranger merely nodded and smiled and did not seem to understand.

"He's a half-wit!" said Sandy.

This report made a sensation in the town, and a party of hunters who were aimed in that direction promised to find the stranger and bring him in. However, what Sandy had done by chance proved very difficult to accomplish by calculation; for the huge breast and sides of Mount Shannon were dressed in virgin forest, and the forest, in turn, was cut across ten thousand times by gulleys, rivulets, and great cañons. It was a labyrinth, and the party of hunters nearly lost their own way without finding the object of their search.

For the sake of convenience, he came to be known as "the man on Mount Shannon" or "the man on Shannon," and in a little while this bulky title was shortened to simply "Shannon."

So he received a name.

The mountain turned white with winter.

For four months people shivered when they looked at its bald head and forest-darkened sides. Then, in the earliest thaw of spring, "Shannon" came down from the mountain bending under a vast load of pelts. He made no less than four separate journeys before he succeeded in carrying down the last of his pelts, and these he turned in at the Bowen store, and he carried back, in exchange, as many loads of flour, sugar, bacon, coffee, a few spices, some rolls of strong cotton cloth, and two pairs of shoes, together with a great deal of powder and lead.

He was surrounded by curious observers every time he appeared in the streets; many questions were written down and given to him, but he answered all requests for information uniformly by shrugging his shoulders and smiling politely. He had bought some books, paper, ink, pens, and it seemed clear that Shannon was determined to stay for a long time on the side of his difficult mountain.

For a month he was busily making these journeys back and forth between his cabin and the town of Lister. If anyone had made bold to follow and observe the hermit on the last of his return journeys toward the mountain, he would have witnessed a strange drama.

Shannon was bending under a hundred-pound pack which would have broken the back of an ordinary man, but he was powerfully made, and six or eight months of toiling over the mountains had given him legs of iron. So his progress was slow, but it was steady enough.

On his second day out, as he went up a trail which was bordered by magnificent silver spruce, set out as though by hand for the sake of their beauty and their broad shade, Shannon paused to put down his pack and drink from a twinkling rivulet, and as he straightened again, and the dizziness cleared from his head after bending, he saw a horse standing in the spotting of the shadows nearby.

It was dying on its feet, dying of old age, he thought when he first saw it, with its ewe neck and pendulous lower lip and dull eyes; for the withers and the hipbones thrust vastly upwards and between the ribs were valleys of shadows. Then he went closer and saw that age could only be one reason. On shoulders, flank, hips, neck, and even across the head ran great welts a whip had made. And along the ribs great knots

8

stood out where the loaded end of the whip had been used when it was found that even the cutting lash—it had slit the skin like a knife—was not enough to persuade the poor creature forward. On either flank was a great crimson place as big as the hand of a man where the terrible rowels had thrust into the bleeding flesh again and again, and from shoulder to hip ran deep excoriations where the rider, with a swinging movement of his leg, had raked his horse fore and aft.

But all of these tokens were minor symptoms; the main horror was yet to be seen. For on the right loin, just where the flesh sank away from before the hipbone, the skin had been gathered up, twisted into a knot, and then through this knot, as a skewer, a rough splinter of wood had been thrust.

Shannon jerked the splinter out, but the horse was so far spent that not even its ears twitched. One ear hung forward; the other lay back on the neck, and there was not a quiver in them as the splinter was withdrawn. And the skin itself had been knotted so long by this perpetual spur thrust that, when the skewer was removed, at first there was no stir, and then only gradually the loose flesh began to crawl into place.

There was a long catalogue of other ills besetting this poor creature, such as deep girth galls under each elbow and gaping saddle sores on either side of his spine.

Shannon hastily tore up some grass and offered it. It was untouched, unsniffed at. He opened the loose mouth and placed the grass inside. Some of it fell out; the rest stuck where it had been placed.

2

HE STOOD A moment to consider.

There is an old saying in the West that after a white man had ridden a horse to a state of exhaustion, a Mexican can extract another day's labor from the failing animal, and after the Mexican has surrendered the work, an Indian can ride the staggering creature for a week. Indian work, Shannon was willing to venture in this case.

He took his rifle, made sure that the load was in place, and stepped aside to take aim, but in taking aim it seemed to him that he was looking at another animal. His narrowed attention shut out the view of that tormented and grotesque body, and the head in itself suggested such a possibility of equine beauty that the hermit lowered the gun in haste.

He opened the horse's mouth again, and then drew in his breath sharply. Old age had nothing to do with the condition of this animal. Its state was all the work of a masterpiece of human cruelty, for one glance at the teeth told Shannon that the horse was a scant five years in age!

He grounded the butt of the rifle with a crash, for this altered the matter. Old age may be pitied, but it cannot be salvaged. Youth is a different matter!

Then he could remember that he had heard or read, somewhere, that hard-worked horses can use a certain percentage of animal food. Even raw meat will sustain them! This reminded Shannon that among the luxuries which composed this last load of supplies he had treated himself to one prime treat—two pounds of butter secured in a tin.

He opened the pack straightway and took forth the tin. In the meantime, the horse made a last great effort and managed to brace its feet a little farther apart. Its head hung still lower down, and shudders of weakness shook the legs.

Shannon lifted the helpless head onto his shoulder, opened the mouth, pulled the tongue out on one side, and down the throat he poured two pounds of choicest butter.

Then he stepped back to watch results. There were no results whatever, apparently. The head hung as low as ever, the eyes were as dead, and the legs shook with the last weakness of life and the coming of death.

He brought water, therefore, and tempted the dying thing with it; there was no response whatever.

He had bought a quart of good brandy as a medicine. Part of this he poured into the empty butter tin; the remaining half he mixed with water and poured this down the throat of the horse.

It was like pouring water on the desert! There was no response. He sent the remaining pint of brandy after the first. Then several quarts of water.

Still there was no sign of life.

He dared not force any more food into that gaunt and tucked-up stomach for fear that the sudden wealth of nutrition might kill as effectually as it will kill a starving man.

There was a sudden groan; the hindquarters of the horse had sunk to the ground in an awkward heap. Vainly he strove to keep his front erect, and, in the last effort of courage, and spirit, pricked his ears as he struggled. Even that effort could not support him and he slumped suddenly to the ground. His head struck it with a heavy jar.

"The end!" thought Shannon.

He actually had remade his pack when, returning to the horse, he found a slight pulse still living in it.

So Shannon made up his mind quickly. The last investments which we can surrender are those which seem made in a lost cause. Where there is no hope, the imagination and the heart fight hardest.

He cut tender young boughs and wedged bedding around the fallen animal. Upon either side of it, he built a strong fire, for the night was beginning and it would be very cold.

After that, Shannon sat under the stars and watched.

Still the horse breathed; still there was a faint and irregular pulse. By firelight

Shannon began to work on those deep spur wounds, on the wide-mouthed saddle sores, on the gouged place where the splinter had been thrust through skin and flesh. It employed him. Presently he was aware that the horse slept, or was dead. He worked on with gentle touches, half convinced that the body upon which his hands were employed was turning cold under them.

So, wearily, the stars began to go out; the great night walked slowly away to the west, and the daylight came cold and dismal and small. With the dawn came a wind, and with the wind were whistling blasts of rain.

Shannon freshened the two fires and put his coat across the back of the horse.

For he still lived. He opened his eyes as Shannon stood before him, and pricked his ears a little.

That to the man was like the waving of victorious flags and the sounding of trumpets.

The rain was coming faster, now, and certainly, in spite of the protection of the coat and the warmth of the two fires, exposure to the cut of the wind and the wet might finish off this poor derelict. Manifestly the cripple could not be moved except through its own power, so Shannon started to urge it up. At last, with infinite difficulty, lifting the bulk of the weight with his own hands, he managed to heave the forequarters up. Then he went behind and tugged and heaved again. At length up came the hindquarters but, like a seesaw, the weak horse instantly fell on his knees.

He had to be raised and steadied again, but now, on braced legs that waved and shook beneath him, he tried to answer the hand of Shannon and go forward. He pricked his ears once more. In his dull eyes came a faint light, as though to indicate that he understood what was wanted and was willing to do his best.

So, a step at a time, as a child moves when it learns to walk, it was brought forward under the high shelter of a spruce with dry ground beneath.

All around him, then, Shannon built a soft and deep bed of softest spruce boughs taken from young saplings. Then he carried water in his hat, and the instant it was brought this poor wreck buried his nostrils deep in the liquid.

He drank and drank again, and when the man brought culled handfuls of seed grass, it was eaten slowly but readily enough. So Shannon had his first real hope!

For a week he lived on that spot. On the fifth day the horse could rise with its own unassisted strength, and go slowly out to graze; on the seventh day Shannon went up the trail and the horse followed like a dog.

Seven days of hand feeding had made little difference in the appearance of the horse except that the mud and the ingrained dust had been worked out of its coat, which appeared now as a dark chestnut, with every hair staring. But the sores and the wounds refused to close, and the belly seemed fully as gaunt as when Shannon forced the first mouthful down the throat of the horse.

Their rate of progress was the most leisurely imaginable. Shannon would walk a hundred yards ahead and then sit down while the chestnut grazed his way to him; and that process was repeated until, at the end of the day, they had drawn a bit farther toward the goal.

That goal was set off to a distance by the roundabout trail which the man was forced to follow, for his usual route, up cliffs and down gulches, would have been quite impossible for the horse. For a whole week they wandered on. There was ample leisure on the way for Shannon to snare game with little gins of his own contriving without using valuable powder and lead; and so they came weaving up the mountainside and at last reached the cabin.

When Shannon lifted the latch and walked in, the chestnut walked in behind him!

On that hint Shannon set to work again. For the building of his cabin he had brought in more logs than actually were necessary, and out of these and some new timber he framed and built a little lean-to against one end of his house. He made it quite high, with a rack of poles stretched across it so that the upper portion could be used as a haymow, for certainly hay must be had if the horse were to live through the winter snows.

Then there was the making of the hay itself.

Just up the valley was a level stretch closely surrounded by timber. Perhaps it was the bed of a glacial lake which, having filled in time with sediment, was now the richest soil imaginable, and here grew tall grass which Shannon felled with a hunting knife. In these days of mowing machines which eat up many acres in a day, scythe work seems ridiculously slow, and a sickle is worse than useless, but many a time Shannon yearned for so much as a sickle. A handful at a time, he advanced across that meadow with his knife. The little meadow seemed like a great prairie. He made gradual inroads here and there, cutting paths to what seemed the choicest grass, and felling that. And every day he brought in the green load of what he had felled.

He began to fall into a regular rhythm of work.

The morning he devoted to walking his trap line, where every trap was a bulky pitfall of his own contriving, since he had no steel traps; and as he walked the line, the horse followed. Then in the afternoon he progressed with his haying—the cutting in the meadow and the shocking of the daily cut near the cabin, and then the storing of the sweet, cured grass in the loft of the horse shed. Furthermore, there was much time to be spent on the chestnut, grooming him, caring for his wounds.

Many a day went by with no change in the horse except a gradual recovery of strength and spirit. But finally, one day, there was a noticeable change, and from that day onward the horse took on flesh and his wounds closed as if by magic.

Whether it was that his thin, starved blood first needed to be recruited before his body could swell out to its old strength, or that it required all this time, before he could assimilate nourishment properly, Shannon could not tell. He only knew that there was this miraculous alteration overnight, and then a daily change in the appearance of the chestnut.

Once the change began, it progressed with wonderful speed. It was almost like the drawing of a new horse each morning, and by degrees Shannon could see that he had picked up no common animal.

He could have told that before. A common nag could never have clung to life as this tormented creature had done, but now it waxed greater. The belly grew sleek first of all. The neck was arched with pride and muscle. Then the lips grew firm and the muzzle square, while fire entered the eyes. After that the quarters and the shoulders filled, the loins were arched across with mighty muscles, and last of all the saddle began to be lined with new flesh and the lofty, staring ridge of the backbone became a beautifully sweeping curve.

The attic now was crammed and hand-packed tightly with good hay, and Shannon had hours to spend at his books, or at his writing, if he would. He rather chose to spend those hours with the horse.

He had invested such a long agony of time and labor in the creature that it was almost more of a child than a beast of the field, and as a mother pores over a child at play, so Shannon could sit for hours, contented, and watch the beautiful young stallion in his comings and in his goings. To watch him eat was a profound pleasure, almost as if the body of the man were being nourished; when he drank, he thrust in his muzzle above the nostrils and gulped the snow water deeply, and a famine fever in Shannon's soul was quenched. Or again, the chestnut galloped through the meadows or raced with a wild recklessness through the trees, dodging them with a cat-footed agility. And it was to the man almost as though he himself had raced and leaped and swerved through the woods!

There was no longer need for him to walk the long round of his traps. He could ride the horse. There was neither halter nor bridle required. A touch of the hand or a pressure of the knee was sufficient. Life in the mountains was becoming easy and joyous, and when Shannon thought of that, he would bow his trouble-marked forehead and ponder the future in a great dread. We cannot have beauty and joy without some shadow being cast from the brightness—without the fear of loss, at least.

Then what he dreaded happened, and the horse was lost to him.

3

THIS WAS HOW it happened.

The day had been long, for at the first dawn the stallion began to paw and Shannon went in wrath to chastise it, but when he opened the door and saw the lifted head and the joyous, fearless eyes of the horse, his heart melted. He put out his hand to the white-starred brow, and speech seemed to rise and swell in the throat of Shannon, though never a word was uttered.

He let the chestnut out to frolic in the pleasant morning. And all the day was filled from that moment with work. The traps were crowded. A coyote was in one fall;

a wolf was in another, and for his scalp the bounty would be anything between ten and fifty dollars—a veritable prize Then, in a third, he found a mountain lion, such a prey as he never had dreamed of winning, and now taken, he had no doubt, by sheerest accident.

All these were killed, then, and they must be skinned. By patience and much study of the problems, he had learned a good deal about skinning, but he never could rival the deftness of a trained worker. Therefore, when at last the carcasses were disposed of and the pelts were framed and on the stretchers, Shannon had no interest in food. He had some jerked venison, swallowed a cup of coffee, and sat down in his doorway to watch the stallion in the meadow, stalking a crow as though in hope to catch and eat it. The wise crow enjoyed the game. It fed in the meadow, or pretended to feed there, with back turned until the stallion pounded. Then a flirt of the wings drove it ahead or side-wise to settle once more in apparent unconcern.

The heart of Shannon was eased from the thought of labor. He lighted his pipe and through the drifts of pale, fragrant smoke he watched the sun slip down in white fire behind the western trees. Then the color began. The whole arch of the sky quivered with it. The stream that slid down the ravine was purple and pink and gold. And since the crow had flown off to bed, the stallion came closer and only made a pretense of grazing while from time to time it raised its head and looked into the face of the master or up to the great flaring vault of the sky, as though drawing wise deductions about the heavens above and this kind god who had descended to the earth to bring mercy where no mercy had been.

At that moment came the tragedy.

The stallion leaped suddenly around, and when Shannon looked in turn he saw a rider on a foaming, staggering horse break from the edge of the woods and rush down on them. Twice he turned his head and looked behind him at the forest he had just left; then he saw the chestnut and threw up both hands in such a gesture of joy as Shannon never had seen before.

"I've got to have him," shouted the stranger. "I'll leave this one—the best thing you ever threw a leg over. Do you want boot? Here's a hundred!"

There was no answer from the mute lips

of Shannon; but when he saw the other leap to the ground, tear saddle and bridle from his beaten mount, and then go toward the stallion rope in hand, Shannon went into the cabin and came out again, rifle in hand.

He saw a game of tag in progress, and the stallion was easily winning until he saw his master in the doorway and fled to him as if for protection. That instant the rope darted snakelike from the hand of the stranger, and the chestnut was snared. The rifle rose to Shannon's shoulder and he drew a steady bead with a hand as strong and quiet as a rock.

He saw down the sights a lean and handsome young face, sun-browned, tense with anxiety and haste, and such a wealth of life gleaming from the eyes and quivering in the lips that Shannon lowered the rifle again; he could not fire even at a thief.

Like magic, saddle and bridle had been slipped upon the stallion and the youth was in the saddle. Again he glanced over his shoulder at the darkness of the trees, while the stallion stood straight up and neighed loudly and swerved toward Shannon in an agony of fear. The cruel spurs went home.

It seemed to Shannon that they were driven into his own sides, and the horse leaped away lightly into the woods beyond.

Then all the little ravine was filled with tumult. A dozen sweating, straining, staggering horses, driven on by whip and spur, came out of the trees and swarmed into the open ground.

"There's the horse! He's near!" some shouted.

And then one whose hat had been torn off in the race through the woods, so that his long gray hair blew over his shoulders, said quietly, "He's changed to a fresh horse. That's old Shannon. But how could he have got a horse from Shannon? Where did Shannon get one?"

They came to Shannon, pouring out questions like water from a miraculous pitcher. Had the fugitive secured a fresh horse? In any case, in what direction had he gone? Was he wounded?

They found Shannon seated in his doorway, his head upon his hand, and never a word of reply did they get.

"Why do you talk to a deaf mute?" said he of the gray hair.

And rapidly he scratched on a piece of paper: "We want Terence Shawn. If you can put us on his trail, there is a fat reward for you.

He placed that paper before Shannon; still there was no response.

So he took it again and wrote in large letters: "One thousand for you!"

When Shannon saw this, he raised his head at last and the sheriff saw such grief and pain that he stepped back and waved his men to him.

"Leave the old chap alone," said the sheriff, though indeed he was an older man than the hermit. "We got to work this trail out ourselves. Scatter, boys, and cut for sign!"

They scattered obediently. Here and there they poured among the trees; then a sudden shout, and the chase streamed away at the point where Terence Shawn had disappeared.

So Shannon was left alone in the darkening evening, with only the beaten turf to tell of what had been there, and in the place of the stallion, a down-headed, beaten horse, with blood-stained flanks and heaving sides

He went slowly toward it. Indeed, there was no kindness or mercy in the heart of Shannon now, but rather in order to occupy his hands, he began to walk the refugee up and down, cooling it slowly.

The full darkness descended. The horse stumbled and coughed behind him, but then by degrees it freshened a little. It no longer pulled back so heavily on the reins, and Shannon led it to the edge of the creek and watched it drink.

It was midnight when he put it in the shed where the stallion had been kept; but it seemed to Shannon that this substitution was worse than a total loneliness, as one feels who takes an adopted child in the vain hope that it will ease the pain when a favorite son has died.

However, that worn-out animal gave him some sort of occupation during the next few days; it was a strongly made bay, with legs that told of much good breeding, and a small head, beautifully placed. Shannon found it child's play to bring the bay around, and in four days it was full of life again.

However, he had not the heart to labor over it as over the chestnut; it would follow him readily enough, come at his whistle, give him a mount when he worked his trap line, but still there was a vast gulf between this and the other.

So life for Shannon settled back to the same empty grimness which had been its characteristic before the chestnut was found and saved.

Autumn was coming, the early autumn of the mountains. He began to find thin mists of ice in the early morning around the edges of the pools. The leaves turned and commenced to fall.

And Shannon resolutely pursued his silent way.

The horse shed was given a small addition which was filled to the top with neatly corded wood, felled and chopped into lengths in the neighboring woods, and then carried in on the hermit's back: for he did not make the mistake of improvidently felling the nearest trunks and making a shambles of his own front yard. All his immediate surroundings remained as wild as ever—only the little cabin was placed between wild meadow and wild woodland, but otherwise Nature was left to her own free, tremendous ways.

Then Terence Shawn came again.

4

THAT EVENING THE stone oven barely had
been fired up and Shannon was busy with
his cookery when the bay whinnied, and
then through the flicker and distant gleam
of the flames, he saw a horseman coming
up the little valley. He swung down from
the saddle and, stepping into the dim circle
of the light, revealed himself as that same
lean and handsome cavalier, Terence
Shawn.

Shannon went past him with a rush, but
the horse to which he stretched out his
hand merely threw up its head and went
uncertainly back.

It was not the stallion; it was a beautifully
made gray, now darkened with sweat, and
standing slouched—exhausted, as all of
Shawn's horses seemed to be when they
came into this valley.

The latter was already busily exam-
ining the bay, and nodding his satisfaction.

"Here's fifty," said Shawn. "And if you
can remake a horse as fast as this, you'll
get money out of me like water out of a

well, old-timer. Hand me something to eat. I don't care what—I've got to go on."

Shannon took the fifty, entered his cabin, and came again. Into the hands of Shawn he put not only that last sum, but also the hundred of the first day, which the outlaw had flung on the ground before the shack.

Shawn stood up, so startled that he dropped from his hand the skewer of wood on which he had been toasting a bit of venison. He stared at Shannon; he searched for words; and then, realizing that speech was useless, he scratched rapidly on paper: "I've taken your horse and left you another with boot. The stallion is a grand one, but not good enough to ride forever. If a hundred wasn't enough, what do you want?"

Glooming, the hermit stared at these words, then passed back the paper with no added word, and went on with his cookery in that same deadly silence.

Terence Shawn sat down where the shadows were thickest, with his back to a boulder which had rolled down here from the forehead of Mount Shannon some forty or fifty millenniums before. Now moss was gathering around its lower sides, and on its cracked and seamed poll where dust and leafmold had settled in the rifts, a scattering of hardy grass and dwarfed shrubbery grew up, never more than a few inches high. How many more thousands of millions of years, thought Terry Shawn, before time and the little prying fingers of winter ice would crumble that heavy mass away and the rivers would carry it down to the sea! Now it sat here in the ravine like an eternal stranger. And so it was, he thought, with this mute hermit. He was dressed in the tatters of any mountain vagabond, and he was set here in the midst of the wilderness, but clothes and position changed him hardly more than the moss and the stunted grass changed the mighty boulder. Both were out of place.

It seemed to Shawn that never had he seen so lofty a forehead, so still and gloomy an eye. Neither sickness nor years could have marked a face as this was marked. It might be the long curse of deafness and silence, but it seemed to Shawn more a trouble of the mind.

There was little reverence or awe in the soul of Terence Shawn. But reverence he felt now, and awe, and a growing shame. Most of all, he was bewildered, for this was an experience outside of all his former knowledge of life and men. If he had taken freely from the strong, like some bandit of the old golden days of romance, he had given as freely to the weak. The banker might well tremble for the safety of his vaults, when he thought of Terence Shawn, but no poor man had ever been troubled. If he took a night's lodging here and a meal there, he paid threefold, and that was why sheriff and deputy rode vainly on his trail. They encountered only people who "didn't know." They failed to see Shawn go by. They had not noticed his direction.

But here, it seemed, was a man who could not be paid for his loss with cash. It appeared to Shawn that the hermit had passed him like a father going to welcome his son. But the stallion was not there, and he had turned back, buried in gloom.

So much Shawn could see, even if he could not understand it, and he was increasingly troubled. To him, hard cash had been the open-sesame. It had never failed before. And now he felt that his pockets were empty, no matter how many closely packed bills of currency were lining them.

He looked back through the shadows to his mount of today. He had stripped the saddle and bridle from it, and after a drink and a roll it was grazing on the verge of the firelight. It was a good horse, a sound horse, a fast horse, well tested for strength and endurance, and surely there was little choice to be made between it and the stallion, say.

Yet the difference existed.

Now, thinking hack, Shawn could remember how the chestnut had taken him down from Mount Shannon and left the sheriff and all of the sheriff's men and their flying horses floundering hopelessly behind him. If a horse was a tool to Terence Shawn, when he rode the stallion he knew that he was employing a most efficient instrument. And this helped him to realize the truth—that the horse was something more than a brute beast in the eyes of the hermit.

So he fell into a mood of reverie and wonder. There was no childish, maudlin emotion about this; instead, the out-law was aware of something profound and grand.

He made no effort to communicate with the hermit again, but in the first hint of the dawn he was gone once more, riding the first horse which he had brought to the man of the wilderness.

It danced down the valley with him with

the utmost lightness and shook out its kinks with five minutes of complicated and earnest bucking.

Then away it swarmed, weaving through the woods and the gulleys with such power that Shawn could not recognize the mound which, not long before, he thought he had wrung dry of all strength forever.

Straight down from the hills went Shawn, flying back on the same course from which he had recently retreated, and he knew that he was flying in the face of danger. He went with what care he could, but he had come into a region most difficult to be traversed with any secrecy during the day. For the hills were open and rolling, there were not many thickets, and the woods were composed of big trees in small groups, so that one could generally look among the trunks of a grove and see the sky on the farther side.

It was dangerous, but as often before in his life, he trusted to luck and to speed to get him past enemies before they knew he was there. While he was cantering past one of these groves, he saw a glimmer of light move in the verge of the trees, and he swung in the saddle, with a Colt poised.

A tall man had already stepped out, with a Winchester thrown into the crook of his arm; and he waved a cheerful greeting. Shawn swerved rapidly in to him.

"What's up, Joe?" he asked.

"Aw, they're swarmin' again," said Joe in casual answer. "You got 'em smoked out again. They're swearin' all the things that they'll do to you, kid.'

"They're hot?" queried the outlaw.

"They're nothing but."

"I don't see why," suggested Shawn.

"Maybe they got no reason," answered the tall man, as Shawn led his panting horse into the darkest center of the trees and loosened the girths. "Only the story that I heard was that when Bowen of the General Merchandise Store come home the other night he found a gent sitting with his daughter on the front porch. Is that right?"

"I dunno," answered the other noncommittally.

"It had the sound of nothin' but Terry Shawn," insisted the mountaineer. "Bowen says to his girl, Who's that with you, Kitty? I can't see in the dusk, here.'

" 'I dunno,' says Kitty. 'This gentleman says that he's waiting for you."

"Then the gent stood up."

" 'I was waiting for you, Bowen,' says he, 'because I had swore that I'd come to pay a call on you. I swore it the day that Chet Lorrain was railroaded to the gallows by your damned high-paid lawyers. I swore to Chet before he died that I'd call on you and see whether you'd got any claim to keep right on living. My name is Terence Shawn,' says you.

"This here little announcement made the girl screech, and old man Bowen he curled up and reached for his gun, but he changed his mind.

" 'All right,' says you, according to the story, 'I ain't going to do what I came down to do. Because, while waitin', I have been able to see that you have got a real reason for deservin' to live, y'understand?'

"And then you said good night to the girl and beat it. Is that the true story, kid?"

"Suppose that it is," said the outlaw. "Why should it make people boil over like this? What harm was there?"

"Harm?" shouted Joe. "Man, man, mean to say you dunno that it's better to kill a man and have done than to shame him and let him try to get even afterwards? Old Bowen is raving around and swearing that he'll make a saddle out of your tanned hide."

"Is that all that bothers these people?" asked Terence Shawn in real amazement. "I tell you, Joe, take things by and large, I can't figure men and their ways. They just nacheral have got me beat!"

"Have they?"

"They have."

"It's because you're a simple, honest, and lovin' soul," declared Joe with profoundest irony. "Come on to the shack with me and have a snack of something to eat; your belly is always, empty. And then you can explain some things to me.

5

THERE ARE WAYS and ways of preparing beans, as everyone knows, and if you have any doubt as to the methods of serving them, look at any pork and beans advertisement. But Shawn's way was unique. He simply sliced away the top of the can and drank off the contents, the can poised in one hand and a formidable and ragged-edged chunk of pone balanced in the other.

He kept silence. Joe was talking excitedly,

but Shawn, with the meditative eyes of one who eats, viewed the far horizon.

"D'you hear me?" barked Joe.

"What?"

"I say, what in hell brought you right back into this mess so soon after you raised it?"

"Well," said Terry, searching idly for a reason, "I wanted to see the girl again. I wanted to apologize for swearin' in her presence."

"You lie," said Joe with a calm surety.

"I gotta be goin'," said Terry with a start.

"Wait half an hour, kid. It'll be near dusk then, and you can slide along through the hills as safe as can be."

Shawn made no answer. He went on into the open.

There he took his horse and drew up the cinches.

"You know that sucker Dick Clover?" inquired Shawn, still with his mind afar.

"Him and me went to school together," said Joe.

"You're friends?"

"None better. We only used to fight on weekdays. Sundays we rested, like the Good Book says.'

"I done Dick Glover a good turn the other day," said Mr. Shawn.

"How come? I didn't hear him asking no special praise down on you the last time I seen him."

"Which was when?"

"This morning."

"Where?"

"Hereabouts. He was with the posse. All he wants of you is the hide. The rest can have the innards."

"There's gratitude," said Terry Shawn, striking a thoughtful attitude.

He added with a sigh, "You know, Joe, people have got me beat so bad that I pretty near give up!"

"What? Booze?"

"Hope," said Shawn. "I pretty near give up hope. I always been saying to myself that one day I'll settle down fine and sober and be a credit to some lucky town, y'understand?"

"Go on," said Joe, yawning shamelessly.

"But now that I come to think it over," he said, "I dunno that it's worth while. Being bad is easy. Just live nacheral and you're sure to raise hell. But doing good— that's the stickler and that's what breaks my heart. I'm like a little kid, Joe. I just don't understand!"

"My heart, it sure does bleed for you," said Joe, rubbing his chin with knuckles hard as flints.

"You take Bowen," explained the outlaw, putting his foot in the stirrup. "Now there is that fat sucker comes home and finds a gent waiting all ready to kill him, and roll his damned fat body down into the gulley and chuck twenty ton of slip rock down on top of it. I had the place all picked out, Joe," said Shawn sadly.

"By God," said Joe. "I'm gunna bust out cryin' when I think what you've given up, kid."

"But I don't kill him," said the outlaw. "I let him crawl away, the measly skunk, and I say no more about troublin' him."

"No," said Joe, "you never would understand. There's a gent that's always stepped into the shoes of God Almighty the minute that he stepped inside the pickets of his front gate. And along you come and show him up to be a damn fourflusher. And the one you pick to show it in front of ain't nobody but the person that is the nearest and the best thing he's got—or that anybody's got. I mean Kitty Bowen! And still you can't understand!"

"Ah," murmured the other, "perhaps you're right. You could always cut for sign wonderful, Joe. Stand still, you damned lop-headed son of a lightning rod!—But the other thing," went on Terry Shawn, after this brief notice to his horse, "the other thing that cuts me up the most is about your old friend, Dick Glover."

"My boyhood chum?" assented Joe, and spat noisily upon the ground.

"There's a gent," said Shawn, "that I positively benefited, the other day."

"How come, would you mind saying?"

"Well, I come along in the need of a horse, and riding one that David Harum couldn't of faulted, a hellcat on wheels, he was. I says to myself, Where shall I leave a grand horse like that and take up another? Because no matter where I go, I'm sure to leave a better horse than I take. Well, I could have drifted over and taken Sim Peter's roan mare, or around to Galways' in the draw and got his brown gelding that talks three languages and runs like thunder. But I happened to think of a nice hardy colt that Dick Glover had, and I said to myself that Dick and me had never been

41

particular good friends, so why not start right in now and put him on the list? I did it, Joe. I dropped over and cut his horse out of the corral and I strapped down my chestnut and left him in the place of the fresh one. Now, Joe, the next thing I hear is that Dick Glover is on my tail and trying to have my scalp. It's hard, Joe!" sighed the outlaw. "And there's no pleasing of men. The best way is just to hold 'em up, rob 'em, and let 'em feel friendly because you took their money and not their hide. Joe, I'm plumb disgusted. I got half a mind," he added gloomily, "to cut loose from these here diggings and strike away in a new direction."

Joe, during the latter part of this moving speech, had been busy working the corner of a cut of Star tobacco and now he continued his silence for a long moment as he brought off a huge section and stowed it with difficulty in one capacious cheek.

"You said it was a chestnut?" asked Joe at last.

"It was," said Shawn. "And I ain't surprised that you know about it, Joe. A horse like that—every puncher on the range would be breakin' his heart for him after a few days!"

"Bones!" said Joe, spitting at a stone and missing it narrowly.

"What you mean?"

"You said hearts. I said bones."

"What's your drift, Joe?"

"I said that horse would break more bones than he ever would have a chance to break hearts!"

"You're wrong," answered the outlaw complacently. "He's a lamb. I never come across one like him. Went like silk, and I never had to touch him with a whip or a spur all the way down from the hills. It was like being tied onto a wind. Let him go and it was like sailing a kite. You just touched the high spots. Slow him up, and he come back into your hand as smooth and as soft as your own bandana handkerchief." Mr. Shawn cast about him for more eloquent expressions, for there was an odd light of disbelief in Joe's eyes.

"You could put that horse," said. Shawn, "in a corner and tell him to stand, and he'd stand all day. You could put him outside your door and he'd watch it like a dog. He was a horse that you could of sat down and had your coffee with in the morning. I used to read the newspaper to him," added Terry Shawn, warming to his work.

"Now what you got to say, you damn lantern-jawed son of trouble?"

He sat in his saddle and grinned amiably down upon Joe, who answered with the same thoughtful seriousness. "There is gifts that can't be got by study," he began. "You gotta have a talent for 'em before you start. You gotta have a head start, so to speak. And then you got to keep right on cultivating. I mean, to get the sort of a gift that you got, kid."

Young Terence Shawn canted his handsome head a little. "What's that?" he asked expectantly.

"I seen some grand men in my day," said Joe. "Right back in my village there was one of the most world-beatingest men you ever heard of; and down in Mexico I met a couple of gents with the real native talent. But I tell you, Terry, that when you open up and sort of get into your stride, there ain't anybody like you at all. You stand off there by yourself."

"Shut up!" commanded Shawn. "Stand off for what?"

"For grand, gray-bearded, mossy, granite-faced, cloud busting lying," declared Joe. "I gotta kind of reverence for you, kid. Damned if I ain't! When I hear you open up on one of your yarns, I wish that I could put it down in short hand. When you die, I'm gunna get famous repeating things that you've said."

"Humph," said Shawn without wrath. "Go on, you slab-sided sap. Go on and get the poison out of you. What's wrong with what I've said? I might draw in my ears about reading the newspaper to him. Nothing else!"

Joe spat again, and again he missed his mark.

"You know Chuck Marvin?"

"Aw, don't I!"

"Can he ride?"

"About the best on the range—bar one," said Shawn with a shameless assurance.

Joe could not help a faint smile.

"I was over to see a little party the other day," said Joe. "It was Chuck Marvin, who'd come three days to take a ride on a chestnut horse that a Mexican has got over to Lister—"

"Damn it," said young Shawn, "I'm talkin' about a horse that I left with—"

"Keep yourself in line," said Joe, "and wait for your turn. I say that I seen Chuck Marvin workin' and laborin' on that chestnut—"

45

"He's a grand man to rake a hoss," admitted Shawn with some jealousy in his voice.

"Rake hell!" exclaimed Joe. "The only use he had for his spurs was to sink 'em into the cinches and wish to God that they were fishhooks, and, if they had been, the chestnut would of pulled his legs off. Chuck, he could hardly keep his head tied onto his neck. First he banged one shoulder and then the other; then he tried to sink his chin through his breastbone, and after that he tried to hit the small of his spine with the back of his head. He kept a good hold to the pommel and the cantle, too. But pretty soon his wrists they begun to give way. It was just plain, ordinary, out-and-out bucking, kid. There was a dash of sun-fishing throwed in at the end, but I can tell you that the chestnut was just sort of getting warmed up to the work!"

"It's another horse," insisted Shawn with irritation. "Glover—"

"Aw," said the tall man, "Glover, he tried to keep the horse, but a greaser in town seen it and claimed it, and had ten pals to swear it was his and stole from him a couple of months ago. He knew its brand, its name, blood lines, and everything else about it, and the judge had to pass the horse on to him before Clover even had a chance to get the pony shod—"

"Pony?" said Shawn, with a rising anger.

"No," said Joe, "they didn't get him shod. They took him down there and they started. But they only had eight men and ropes to handle him, and so, of course, he knocked the anvil, smashed the forge, and spilled fire everywhere, and while they was putting out the fire, he just took off the rear end of the shop and chucked it out into the pasture, and then he walked off to enjoy the sun. However, the greaser has him, and he's offering the horse to anybody that can ride him. The only thing is that you got to pay five dollars a throw."

"By God!" said Terence Shawn. "It beats me! He's the sort that would eat out of the hand of a baby."

"He still would," said Joe. "And you could let him walk over ten babies and he never would touch one of them. And he stands in his pasture there and makes love to everybody that goes by. But if you start to make him do anything—that's a little different!"

"Bah!" said Shawn. "I can make that horse—"

"You can't. You didn't know him. He wasn't growed up the last time that you met him. He never had even been inside of a kindergarten, but now he's a damn college graduate, a doctor and a lawyer and a minister rolled together. They call him Sky Pilot, over in Lister now!"

He spat again, and the little stone turned brown.

After a moment of thought, Mr. Shawn changed the conversation.

"When you go to town, get me a side of bacon, will you?"

"I sure will."

"Here's the price."

"I don't need fifty dollars for a side of bacon," said Joe.

"I got no change, and I'm in a hurry. I'm gunna go get me the chestnut, the Sky Pilot, Joe!"

Joe folded the bill and slipped it into his money belt.

"You go right on, son," said he. "I don't think that you'll ever come back to bother me for the change out of this here!"

6

THE COOL OF the dusk was beginning; and now the kid galloped briskly away, taking the straight road for Lister. He had not had that goal in his mind when he started, but wherever the horse was, there was his duty.

For now he felt he must restore the horse to the old man, and he wondered to himself with a ruminative mind how difficult the task would prove when he approached the town and found the pony.

He would far rather that it should be in the hands of any rancher, no matter how rich or how well he kept the chestnut guarded. For such men could be deceived, but a fellow of the type of this particular Mexican—that was a different matter. It would be like entering a wolf's den to steal away the cubs without slaughtering the mother first. A horse which brought in five dollars a ride was a veritable treasure. Neither day nor night would the fellow be away from the stallion.

Purposely he had not asked the location in which the chestnut was kept. He wished to draw that information from another quarter and the thought of the coming interview made Terry Shawn tilt his head a bit to one side, with an expression which was close to sheer deviltry.

So he went on toward Lister cheerfully, not allowing his thoughts to roam too far into the future. Indeed, there never was a great deal of time for reflection in the life of Terry Shawn, for he never settled down to a lonely moment without having to listen up and down the wind, like a hunted wolf. With the difference that this wolf rather enjoyed the hunt.

He swung out of the dark, at last, above the town, and he examined it with a complacent satisfaction, almost as one might who has painted a picture. For he knew Lister so well that all of the lights had a meaning to him, and he even could pick out the dim glimmer of Mrs. Dodge's lamp from the broader and clearer flare of Mrs. Thompson's window across the street. He knew Lister. He had to know it; for Lister was his base of supplies.

So he studied the familiar spot, with a perfect content, and then he drifted off to one side. He left the lights of the little town behind him, entered a little valley and presently came through the trees on the site of a considerable ranch house.

He listened once, he listened twice, and then boldly he rode forth from covert.

Behind the ranch house, from their own quarters, the cowhands were raising a song; a dog slipped from the shadow of a brush patch, sniffed at the legs of Mr. Shawn's horse and disappeared again; and Terence Shawn went on to the farther corner of the building.

There he stooped from the saddle and looked in through the open kitchen window. A vast Negro woman was waddling about the room. All the disorder of after supper appeared in the heaped pans which strewed the sink. She had a benevolent appearance, though be could not decide whether it was an inner content that made her so cheerful or simply the automatic pull of the rolls of fat at the corners of her mouth which made her seem always to smile.

"Hello!" said he.

"Where you talkin' from?" she said, lifting her head and surveying the ceiling. "Has you come down for ol' Aunt Midget angels?"

"Hello," said Shawn.

She located him.

"Hello man" she said. "What you want honey?"

"A great big slice out of that roast ham that you got there on the warmin' shelf."

"Step right inside" said the cook. "Step right inside and help yourself! I hope to Gawd that I ain't turned no hungry stomach from my door. Nor neither would Missus Bowen be wantin' me to."

Shawn obeyed the invitation literally, stepping out of the stirrups and through the window.

"You-all been riding quite a piece," said Aunt Midget. "Set down and shove your feet under that table. I'll feed you honey!"

"Everybody gone from home?" asked Shawn.

"Everybody" said Aunt Midget. "They ain't scasely nobody in callin' distance of me except about ten of the boys in the bunkhouse. You hear 'em tunin' up?"

She jerked her thumb over her shoulder toward the window, through which poured the strains of hoarse and timeless music from the cowpunchers.

And Terence Shawn smiled. He could not help understanding this hidden reference to the cook's help so close at hand—in case Terence should turn out a robber.

However, she made no significant pause, but went blandly on in her good-natured, husky voice, indicating that the family had gone into Lister to attend a dance in the town lecture hall.

"And what be your business in this part of the world?" asked Aunt Midget, piling a heap of chops on the plate before her guest.

"I been hearing a good deal about a bang-up sort of a horse around here," said he. "I mean a horse that some Mexican has got—and him that rides him can take him."

"You mean the Sky Pilot?" she asked. "I heard about him, too. He's as good as an epidemic to the doctors. He lays up a man a day, as regular. And nothin' small and mean about him. No cracked ribs and bruises and dislocations, and such. When the Sky Pilot gets busy, he finishes up. Busted hips is special with him," sighed Aunt Midget, "and fractured skulls he is extra fond of doing, but slammin' them on the ground so hard that their insides turns to custard and gets all scrambled up, and their brains is all knocked into con-cussions, that's his main line. He's a lovely horse! And you'd be comin' down to ride him, young man. Is that it?"

"A man can have a try," suggested he. "There's no harm in that, Aunt Midget."

"There ain't," she said. "You can't no more than lose your life and we all got to die some day. Only it ain't just the sort of death that I'd be pickin' you out to choose."

"No?" he said politely, swallowing a great draught of coffee. "How would you lay me out, Aunt Midget? How would you figger that I'd be trimmed up and put on the shelf?"

She turned and looked down at him with a degree of penetration which gave her almost a disdainful look.

"Guns!" said Aunt Midget.

"Guns?" he cried. And he held up his hands.

She nodded, so that her hanging double chin wagged to and fro.

"You hardly ever seen such things, most like," she said.

"I'm a quiet man," he declared.

"All the bad ones is," she answered with a perfect assurance. "A fire that roars ain't the fire that does the work. The fire that just gives you a quiet little hiss, that's the one that burns the bread in the oven and melts the top off of the stove.

She shook her head again, and again the double chin wobbled.

Terence Shawn narrowed his eyes at her.

"Suppose that you're right?" he suggested.

"Oh, I'm right."

"You don't seem scared, Aunt Midget."

"Scared?" she cried. "Scared of a man?"

Her strong bass laughter boomed and flooded through the kitchen until the pans heaped in the sink trembled with the vibrations.

"I have swep' out a whole roomful of 'em," said she. "I have started forty of the wildest and the most man-killingest on the run with one ladle of soup in their faces—"

And, as she spoke, she scooped out a dipperful from a great black pot at the rear of the stove and waved it in the air. Shawn shrank away with startled eyes.

But she, without spilling as much as a drop, returned the ladle to the pot. She was still chuckling.

"Scared?" said she. "I hope no man is ever gunna scare Aunt Midget. The good

Lawd help the man that ever tries to! But a little narrer, weazened-up, starvation boy like you—"

Her laughter boomed again to complete her sentence, and Shawn flushed a little. He had a vague and boyish desire to announce himself in all the splendid dignity of his crimes and his daring deeds, but he restrained the impulse and smiled instead.

"I won't try," he said. "I wanted to talk about a horse and not about guns, Aunt Midget. Where could I find the Mexican?

"That Jose? I dunno. You go down and you ask for the meanest-lookin' man in town and the orneriest and the worst, and that's him. I dunno where he lives."

"You never saw the Sky Pilot bucking?"

"I never seen him pitch one lick," she sighed. "Fact is that it ain't no easy thing for me to go roamin' and ravagin' around the country. When I tried to get into the buck board the other day, the doggone step, it busted away under me. Everything, these days, is made for lightweights and skeletons. They don't take no account of folks with a little substance to 'em!"

And she looked down with sorrow and

56

pride mingled upon her vast and swelling front. He had risen.

"Here, you!" called the cook. "Mr. Outlaw, Mr. Robber, Mr. Horsethief, whatever your name might be, you come back here and sit down and try some of this pudding. It'll be good for what ails you!"

7

MOST COMFORTABLY AT ease with himself and the world at large, Terence Shawn at last departed. Only with difficulty had he been able to close a dollar into the great, moist hand of Aunt Midget, and now he jogged softly through the night.

Before the morning, perhaps Aunt Midget would have cause to revise some of her opinions about the harmlessness of men, for in the mind of Shawn an idea was developing slowly.

He had come to Lister to ask about the horse and hear an answer from one definite pair of lips. So far, he had had no chance to get the correct answer from any other, and though he had no doubt that he could learn what he wished from the first chance-met passer-by on the darkness of the road, still he was inclined to persist in his first determination and take the reply from one only.

And that was none other than Kitty Bowen.

She had rested in his mind ever since his last meeting with her. She was no classic beauty. Her mouth was too large, except when she smiled and dimpled. Her nose was too short, and it wrinkled absurdly when she laughed. But all the rest of her was so perfectly made that it reminded Shawn of a clean-bred horse, a trifle out about the head say, but all the intricate running mechanism set beautifully in hand. So it was with this girl. If she did not hold your eye at the first glance, she surely would hold your ear with the sound of her voice, and, after that, when you looked at her she seemed changed, for one saw less of flesh and more of spirit—more of womanliness, more of a strong and kindly heart.

Ever since his meeting with her, she had lain in the back of the outlaw's mind. And now he had a foolish desire to hear of Sky Pilot through her. He knew that it was a perverse and foolish desire, and yet he could not help being sure that he never would give up the effort to see her until he had accomplished that desire. There was nothing in his mind to say to her, except to make the one question. No doubt she would think him mad as this act deserved to be called, but for some reason, what she thought hardly mattered. He merely wanted to be close enough to see her, breathe of her presence, taste the wine of a delightful personality, and then it would be easier, beyond doubt, to go back to the loneliness, the long rides, the deadly silence of the listening nights among the mountains or on the bare and dangerous face of the plains.

He went straight for the lecture hall.

He knew all about it.

There had been a time when, with no shadow on his name, he had walked freely into that big barnlike building, presented his ticket for two, then drifted off into the dance. In those times he had looked all men in the face carelessly, cheerfully. He looked them in the face still, because he dared not do otherwise. He must search every eye to see where danger lurked.

Opposite, and a little down the street, in the mouth of the dark alley which ran between Duncan's Livery Stable and the Lucas Blacksmith Shop, he sat in the saddle and looked across to the dimly lighted doorway of the hall. The familiar knot of punchers was there, men who had tired of the dance or could not find partners, and who therefore had come out here to look at the stars and guess about the weather and remark that Smith was getting pretty sweet on the Jones girl.

They leaned against the hitching rack on their elbows. They leaned against the wall. They shifted to stare curiously at new arrivals. And suddenly Shawn was glad that he was not of them. They had their world of people, and he had his world of the mountains.

So, almost fiercely, he jogged around the block and tethered his tired horse in the brush just behind the hall.

Two or three young couples were out there, moving slowly, their arms about one another, their heads drawn close together. Love seemed to him like a sickness.

No common sense in what he was about to do, but as one who has put his hand to a work, something drove him on to finish it. The sudden contempt he felt for all these people made him the more confident in going on with the scheme.

He returned boldly to the front of the

building. In the darkness around the first corner, he paused and there brushed himself carefully. He had only a handkerchief for the work, but then he knew where all the dust wrinkles were, and it was not the first time that he had made himself presentable without light or mirror.

His chaps remained behind, hanging over the saddle horn; it left him lighter and surer of foot for whatever might happen.

He stepped on again and turned in through the doorway. There was only a casual turning of heads; what blind fools!

At the ticket window: "How many?"

"One, please."

"That'll be a dollar. You get your supper ticket inside."

And the hands tore off a ticket from the roll without a lift of the head to examine the latest patron.

Then, behind him, Shawn heard a quiet voice among the idlers at the door: "Boys, that was Terence Shawn!"

The ticket seller looked up hastily enough, at that. His cheeks pulled in and his eyes grew big. Both his brown, gnarled hands reached for the cashbox.

One of those brave men who die for their sense of duty.

"It's all right," said Shawn. "I'm not on the warpath—unless I have to be!"

8

Now Shawn turned and looked back, and he considered the narrow passageway that opened upon the street. The single lamp which illumined it gave a smoked and unhappy light, yet it was bright enough to make good shooting, and he knew that, in case of a retreat, he could not come back this way.

He went on briskly up the steps which widened and opened above upon the spacious reception room in front of the dance hall.

There were a full dozen youths loitering here, and every one of them appeared to know him on sight. They gaped; from one set of loosened fingers a cigarette dropped and was allowed to fume unheeded upon the floor. But Shawn went on through the wide doorway and entered the dance hall itself.

Two sets of danger had been passed and lay behind him. Some of those youngsters he had just passed appeared weak and vicious enough to shoot a man through the back, but he dared not turn to glance behind him. What shielded and supported him now, above all, was simply his own calm indifference to the situation in which he found himself.

The dance was in full sway. The floor throbbed underfoot; the very streamers and crosslines of bunting high above swayed and shook with the music and with the dance; and Terence Shawn looked into his own heart and marveled, for he was not moved.

He thought that they seemed not really happy. Here and there he saw a jovial couple, recently become lovers, perhaps, and enthralled still by the marvels of one another.

And then—there were the two people in whom, for obvious reasons, he was most interested. One was the sheriff; and the other was the sheriff's partner, Kitty Bowen.

The regularly concentric circles of the dancing swarm began to deviate and fall into disorder, now. The floor was covered by a weaving and uncertain pattern. Many of the couples had stopped dancing. Some hurried toward their chairs ranged along the four stiff walls. Some huddled together in dense groups, the women gravitating to the inside of these groups, and the men on the outer rims. And even those who continued resolutely to dance were turning their eyes more and more upon that slender young man who stood near the door, one hand upon his hip, his head moving a little as he swept the hall with his calm scrutiny.

So, out of the maze, the sheriff suddenly developed with Kitty Bowen at his side.

The sheriff came striding. He was a fighting man. His jaw was set, and the muscles at the base of it were bulging. His eyes glared. He would have come shooting, beyond a doubt, had it not been that Kitty Bowen was trying to keep up with him—and clutched his right arm to keep pace.

"Terry Shawn!" gasped the sheriff through his teeth. "I—"

"Hello, sheriff," said Mr. Shawn pleasantly. "Now, I call it doggone kind of you to give up your dance to me, sheriff. I'll see you later, old fellow!

And, somehow, he stepped forward and took Kitty Bowen in his arms. The sheriff, dazed, stretched out a detaining hand, but it slipped from the coat of Mr. Shawn, and the poor sheriff stood like a crimson-faced statue, realizing that it must appear that when the long-rider appeared, he, the upholder of the law, had straightway brought a dancing partner to the criminal, and patted the latter kindly upon the shoulder as the two danced away together.

What could he do? The sheriff quite forgot his guns. The affair had been shifted upon another plane of he hardly knew what.

"Are you going to hold up everybody in the room?" Kitty Bowen was asking of her new partner.

"Me?" cried the outlaw. "Why, I just came down for a dance and a chat. I been thinking about you a good deal."

"The music is going all to pieces" said Kitty.

"We'll shake 'em up a little," said the outlaw, and as they were passing the orchestra stand at that moment, he waved cheerfully at the musicians.

They stood up of one accord, as though a gun had been swung in their direction. The music staggered almost to a close, and then it began again with a fresher and truer swing than ever, as though those men of art, appreciating a brand-new situation, were happy to rise to it.

There were few dancers on the floor, now. The crowd was packed in the corners. There were two notes in its voice—one was the sharp high rattle of questions from the girls, and one was the deeper hum of the men as they made stern resolutions.

"I've got about half a minute left," said Terry Shawn. "The sheriff is coming to. He'll have his guns out, pretty soon. I had a question to ask you, Kitty."

She nodded. Her head was turned to the side and raised a little; she seemed to be looking into distance with absent eyes. She seemed to Shawn neither frightened, embarrassed, nor happy, but merely thoughtful.

"I want to know about the Sky Pilot," said he.

"The Sky Pilot?"

"I mean the horse."

"Oh!" she said.

"Where does he hang out with the Mexican?"

"Jose has rented a lot from Jud Makin, and he keeps the chestnut there. What do you want with him, Terry?"

"I got to make a present to a friend," said he, rather inaccurately.

"Did you have to come into the dance hall to ask the question?" she said.

"I'd sat with you, walked with you, talked with you, Kitty; but I'd never danced with you. Besides, I wanted to ask you another question. When can I see you again?"

"I never leave the valley," said she.

"That's what the dog said to the wolf."

"Yes, they want you. Will they ever have you, Terry?"

"Some day they'll have me. But I ought to have a few years left."

"Not if you keep coming to dances."

"It depends on where I have to go to find you."

"I'm going riding tomorrow," said Kitty.

"Which way?"

"Up Lawson Creek."

"What time?"

"Oh, about nine in the morning."

"That's a funny thing," said he. "I was gunna go riding up Lawson Creek myself at that same time."

She looked away from the distance and suddenly and brightly up to him; then she smiled, and the heart of Terence Shawn contracted and then expanded so wildly that all the hanging lanterns in the hall blurred together and the music was multiplied in his ears as though it were the straining of great martial trumpets.

"You'd better jump," said the quiet voice of the girl. "They've blocked the doors, but you could get out that window, there."

"How far is it to the ground?"

"Thirty feet, but there's a shed roof just under the window."

"So long, Kitty. It was a grand dance."

"So long, Terry. I'm glad you dropped in."

He slipped from her.

The sheriff had endured it long enough and now he was coming with a gun in either hand, glimmering wickedly in the lantern light; and everyone else was silent except one girl who had begun to scream, now in a long wail, now in sharp, short cries, so that she reminded him of a train whistling anxiously for a crossing where the signals were wrong.

Terence Shawn dodged through the crowd, and over their heads he tossed a little knot of banknotes into the midst of the musicians. He leaped up, caught the lower sill of the loftily placed window, and swung himself up into the gap.

He stood up against the blackness of the outer night and threw one glance before him at the sloping roof of the shed, then one glance behind him, where the sheriff stood with guns poised, shouting something about surrender.

Fire jetted from the muzzle of one of those guns, and a tinkling shower of glass fell around Shawn. Then he jumped, struck the roof, rolled forward head over heels, and barely caught the outer rain gutter in time to check his fall. The nails worked loose. The gutter stripped off the edge of the roof with a noisy screeching, but Shawn had dropped lightly on his feet to the ground below.

9

WHEN SHAWN STRUCK the ground outside he had no great amount of time left to him. He had barely located the spot at which he had stationed his horse when the rear door of the hall was cast open by the sheriff, cursing savagely because the door had resisted his efforts so long. The shaft of light drove in a wide wedge full upon slender Terry Shawn, and the oaths of the sheriff turned to a wild shout of joy.

He should have fired in silence and saved a split part of a second, for in that precious fraction of time, Shawn leaped to the side into enveloping darkness with two bullets winging wickedly close to his ears.

Then he sprinted for his horse and swarmed into the saddle. A good horse needs no spur at such a time. The fear and the need of its rider send a quiver of fright and eagerness through its body. So, the instant that he felt the weight of Shawn in the stirrups, the horse was running and fighting for his head.

Straight out from Lister he raced, and when there was a breathless mile of darkness between them and the confused lights of the town, Shawn at last managed to get his mount in hand.

When that happened, he swung back in a sharp curve that returned him to the village almost in a straight line.

Trotting his horse softly on, he paused twice in shelter of brush and watched rushing bands of riders storm through the night, beating wildly out from Lister.

He knew why they rode, and he laughed at their speed. The more of them who mounted and galloped in this bitter fashion, the easier would be the task which lay before him.

He knew where the fields of Jud Makin lay and he went to them. There, at the head of the town where the houses thinned and changed to infrequent dottings on the landscape, there was a little shack beside the river. As Shawn slackened his pace and went on more slowly than before, he heard before him the twanging of a guitar. He bent his head; it was Spanish. He drew closer; it was Spanish, to be sure, and it was a ballad relation of the incredible exploits of a bold brigand and his lucky adventures with the purses of men and the honor of women.

Down the bank by the edge of the stream, he threw the reins of the horse and went from it toward the shack, still pausing again and again, and circling until he made sure that the noise of the musical instrument was coming to him from the farther side of the shack.

When he was sure of that, he went forward more surely, and presently he was creeping down every side of the little shanty.

He found the Mexican sprawled in the

doorway, his guitar in his lap, his head against the doorjamb, with the long black hair falling back from it and his face turned pale toward the stars.

The song ended. "And what do you think of it?" asked the voice of Jose.

Shawn bit his lip. This one rascal was apt enough to give him plentiful trouble, but if he had a companion, the work might be almost impossible. Say what men will about the courage or the lack of courage of a Mexican, in the night he makes a very efficient fighter, if he is a fighting man at all. And Terry Shawn knew all about the potentialities of the Mexican who now sat before him. There was no more dangerous man on the southern side of the Rio Grande, and hardly three on the northern side, for that matter.

There was no answer, immediately, to the remark of Jose, and the latter snarled grimly, "Tell me, devil, what do you think of it?"

Still not a voice replied.

Then Jose caught up a blacksnake, and its snaky body curled and whisked out of sight as he snapped it.

"Speak to me! For you can speak if you wish to! Speak to me, you son of the raw north wind and a sandstorm! Ugly soul of tequila, poison heart, witch, will you answer me?"

It turned the blood of the listening man a little cold. It was hard to imagine that a second man was inside the shack, but it well might be a woman whom this brute had persuaded out from the town to share his quarters with him.

The fingers of Terry Shawn began to twitch, and he crouched a little with the strength of his disgust and his anger.

"No," said Jose in a greater passion than before, "you will not speak. Not here. Not now. You save your words. But when the right day comes, then you will speak. When you think that you can damn me, devil! But you are wrong. You are a fool. Always I am your master. I take you in my hand. I bend you, and I make you what I will. Ho! Stand over and give more room to my thoughts, in there!"

With that, he turned on his elbow and struck savagely into the darkness. The answer was a snort and a heavy trampling; and the heart of Shawn was partly relieved and partly thrilled with wonder. It was the horse which lived inside the shanty!

"Jose!" he said.

The Mexican turned as a cat turns when a dog comes suddenly around a corner behind it. He looked venomously up to Shawn, his lean, ugly face all twisted with malice and with terror.

"Ay, ay," he answered slowly, when he had run his eyes over the slender, well-poised form of the outlaw. "Who are you? I am Jose, but who are you?"

"There's my card," said the outlaw, and dropped a five-dollar bill into the lap of the Mexican.

The latter clutched it; then he stumbled to his feet. His sullen voice turned to an easy and droning gush of courtesy.

"I understand, señor," said he. "There are two fortunes for men. There is a fortune by day and there is a fortune by night. Señor, perhaps, has tried already by day. Now he wishes to try the other half of his luck. Is it so?'

He drew closer, and his laughter bubbled with unhealthy pleasure. Shawn stepped back.

"Get the horse out," he said. "Throw a saddle on him and let me have my fling. If I ride him, he's mine, eh?"

"If you ride him?" repeated the Mexican, disappearing into the shack.

Presently he was heard cursing the horse, and alternately chuckling.

"If you ride the horse, he is a present to you. You shall take him and be happy with him, friend!"

He led the chestnut into the starlight.

Certainly, in the hands of Jose, Sky Pilot had not deteriorated in condition. He had the best of food, or else never would his coat have shone in such a fashion; he had a sufficient share of hard exercise, also, given by those who paid for their chances to ride him with dollars first and with broken bones afterwards.

Only in spirit had he altered from the gentle-mouthed and star-eyed creature on which the outlaw had descended like the wind from the mountains. Indeed, that very lack of fire in spirit had been what caused him to misjudge the capabilities of the animal. A little more iron in the soul of the stallion, and he would have guessed the value of what he had ridden that other night. But now, with his ears pricking slowly forward or else quivering back, tight shut against his head, with his eyes glittering and his feet reaching and pawing uncertainly, he looked the very spirit of evil and treachery and danger.

"Amigo," said the outlaw, "tell me why you hate this horse?"

"I have such reasons," said the other, "that I have made a song of them, and one day I'll sing it for you, perhaps—"

He forced himself to stop short, but it was not too difficult for Shawn to fill out the thought. Perhaps when he lay smashed and broken against the ground, long sick and slowly recovering, there would be a chance for him to hear the song of the Mexican in which the story of the Sky Pilot was told at large.

Terry Shawn took thought with some gravity.

If, in fact, he were thrown and hurt so badly that he could not get away from the place, the law would soon have him in its arms. He never could trust to this treacherous Jose to take care of him and nurse him back to health and strength again.

"Stand him out here!" he commanded.

With a half hitch taken cruelly deep and hard in the upper lip of the chestnut, Jose stood the horse in the required spot, where the starlight shimmered more brightly over him.

"He's a devil!" whispered Shawn to himself.

"He is, señor," said the Mexican eagerly. "And who would not like to have a devil for a slave? Who would not like, señor, to cross mountains and desserts on wings, eh?"

"But you, Jose, who would love to rule a devil so well, why don't you ride him yourself, then?"

"I *have* ridden him," said Jose sadly. "But we cannot have the same life given twice. It only can be sold once!"

"Now, what do you mean by that?"

"My meaning is clear. No? Let it go, then, for the important thing is just that you should ride the horse, señor—or else take your fall. Do you see? You have all this field to circle in. That fence is so high that even he cannot jump it—yet. If he does not buck you off or rub you off against the fence, then it will be well with you, señor. You shall have him. Begin, señor. Begin!"

"Hold his head, then," said the outlaw sternly and crisply. "I'll ride him, by God, unless he bucks his jacket off! Are those cinches strong?"

"They are, señor. Try them!"

"If one of 'em breaks, or a stirrup gives way with me, I'll have a gun on you while

I'm falling, Jose, and I'll send your sneaking yellow soul to the hell where it belongs! Hold his head, now.

And, with a single bound, he was in the saddle and had swept the reins into his hand.

The Mexican, in the meantime, had leaned far forward. Now he threw up his hands with a groan that was half fear and half rage.

"It is Señor Shawn!" he cried. "Oh, devil, now you have come to your last day!"

10

THE EXCLAMATION OF Jose seemed in part joyous at the thought that the chestnut was now, perhaps, to be mastered, and in part it seemed anger and fear because the end of his money-making seemed in sight.

Shawn had but the slightest glimpse of that play of emotions in the Mexican's face. The next moment Sky Pilot took control and went straight forward, not like a horse about to show his paces as a skilled bucker, but rather like a racer off the mark his head thrusting out, his ears flattened by speed, his quarters sinking with the power and the lengthening of his stride.

But Shawn gathered that trouble was ahead. He settled himself more deeply in the saddle, though the rapid vibrations of a running horse were the most unsettling thing in the world. The temptation is to rise in the stirrups, lean forward, and let the long loin muscles whip freely back and forth as the horse runs. But Shawn settled deeper and secured his knee grip by turning in his toes a little that slight toeing-in throwing on all the power of the thigh muscles inside the leg. He was gripping hard, and yet, like a perfect horseman, he was giving himself to the motion of the run, to an extent. He sat strongly, but not rigidly, and waited for the shock.

It came, but not exactly as he had expected.

The chestnut left the ground in a broad jump, but he twisted himself a little to the side, and then came down with arched back, dropped head, and rigid legs. So mighty was the impact that the hoofs cut through the hard soil like plowshares; so clean was the impact that Terry Shawn went numb of brain, yet he would have stuck in his place had it not been that the little twist at the end of the leap acted upon him like a fiendish leverage. He was literally peeled from the saddle and sailed on violently through the air.

He might have broken his neck with a fall of half that violence, but Terry Shawn knew all about the fine art of falling.

One should not sprawl, and yet one should be loose. The instinct is to go face down, with fending arms thrust out. But Terry Shawn knew that one must turn the side first, the back if possible, and hit with a roll.

Hard to think of such things when being hurled from a bucking horse.

But, after all, if he had not been able to crowd a great deal of thinking into the split part of a second, he never would have been what he was. He struck the ground rolling, and his fall carried him spinning under the lower bar of the fence.

More than half stunned, his wits reeling, still he was conscious of a shadow leaping after him, of hoofs that beat against the rails, and a cloud of dust swept over him and half stopped his breathing.

It was the chestnut, which had come after him with a tigerish ferocity, and then, realizing that this man could not be reached, went flaunting off around the corral, his head raised as he eyed the top bar here and there.

But that fence could not be jumped. Sometimes a fresh-caught wild horse will try the impossible and hang himself over a rail; but not the most frantic wild horse in the world would dream of tackling this barrier.

Yet the Mexican hurrying, rope in hand, went with an anxious step.

He cursed and berated the horse as he advanced, and Shawn, sitting up with staggering brain, heard a speech somewhat as follows:

"Son of a devil, son of an ass and a yellow mountain goat, you have won again, but you have not beaten me. I come again, and I bring my rope with me. Listen to it, my beautiful! This is music! You have heard it before. You cannot escape. Dance and smash the ground, but you won't smash me. You are afraid, my pretty one, my hellcat, because you see the rope in my hand.

Shawn's eyes cleared a little; he staggered to his feet and now he saw Jose advancing with outstretched arms, a coil of the rope in either hand, feinting first with one and then with another, and the chestnut backed and pranced and danced, looking as savage as any minor lord of hell, to be sure, and quite aware of the danger before him.

He plunged suddenly to the right; the left hand of the Mexican feinted; the horse whirled, and instantly Jose cast from his other hand. But it seemed that the chestnut had a rare mind as well as the muscles of a bouncing rubber ball, for he spun about again, and, leaping from under the evil whisper of the rope, he galloped off to the farther end of the inclosure.

Jose, gathering his rope again into his hands, laughed from sheer excess and boiling-over of anger

"I am coming, nevertheless," he assured the high-headed stallion. "Run from me, and you run from your shadow. You cannot escape from me, my beauty! Steady, therefore! Stand patiently. Put out your head for your master.

So he came up again with the stallion; and this time the horse rushed straight ahead, as though frantic with fear. But when the rope shot up, he braced himself to a halt and swerved away from it.

Shawn had picked the thorns of a cactus out of his shoulder. He shook himself like a dog out of water and found that there were no broken bones. Then he climbed the fence and gave Jose his aid. So the two of them managed to corner that clever dodger, and the rope of the Mexican went home around the neck of Sky Pilot. The instant he felt the touch of the rope, he stopped and stood shuddering. What lessons he had learned, plainly he had learned them well.

"Hold his head," said Terence Shawn.

"You ride again, señor?" asked Jose, a sudden burst of admiration warming his voice.

"I ride again. Hold him steady!"

And he leaped a second time into the saddle.

The story began in the same way—a blind rush of speed, a leap into the thin air, a sidewise spin and shock on stiffened legs. But this time the rider clung to his place; he was prepared.

The Pilot, as though disappointed at this result, started on at the softest of jogs, and Shawn studied the silken ease of that movement. He gritted his teeth. All this had been revealed to him on the very first day he mounted the animal, and yet he had closed his eyes against the truth. He had picked up this horse from a hermit among the mountains, and who will dream that a glistening crystal found in the gutter is a priceless diamond, no matter how brightly it blazes in the sun?

At any rate, the horse had gone from him into the hands of the Mexican . . .

These thoughts were interrupted by a sudden burst of fence-rowing done with a neatness and finish that, in the experience of Terry Shawn, put to shame every other talented performer at that line of trade. He felt as though he were riding a section of steel cable, flourished and snapped in the air by some malicious, gigantic hand.

And then, suddenly, the chestnut was trotting on again. The Mexican was shrieking with excitement, dancing and waving his hands.

"The whip, señor! The spur! Now let him taste a master in the saddle!"

But Shawn had not advanced to that stage of confidence. There was something more in the wily brain of this animal. Besides, he wanted a bit of a breathing spell, so that the darkness could depart from his own head. It was as though he had been beaten over the back of the head with a bludgeon.

Then straight into the air plunged the

chestnut and floundered backwards. Of all the tricks of man-killing horses, none is so deadly as this, and Shawn barely had time and wit to jerk himself out of the saddle as the horse fell. Catlike, the chestnut spun up to his feet again, but, like a cat also, Shawn had leaped to his place in the saddle and clung there.

Once more into the air and down again. Three times the stallion repeated this maneuver, and each time Shawn escaped by a narrower margin.

After that, the Pilot went on with his soft jog trot, shaking the bridle and patently thinking. It reminded Terry Shawn of a battle out of the days of his childhood, when he had stood up to the son of a blacksmith in his home town—a lean, tall, hard-muscled boy with a blue eye as cold as the eye of a fish. Twenty times he had rushed that lad, and twenty times he had been received with a new trick, a new cunning shift that baffled him. However, in the end he had managed to come to close quarters, and then a few minutes of delightful punching laid the stalwart lad on his back, defeated. So it might prove with the stallion!

He barely had reached that hopeful conclusion, when Sky Pilot began to spin like a humming top. There was no bucking. Simply an amazingly rapid revolution, so that he seemed to have been fixed upon a pivot and spun there.

His head reeling, his body wavering, Shawn gritted his teeth and prayed for success. The star points had turned into long, gleaming circles of light. The trees were vast streaks of blackness. And the Mexican had been multiplied by ten and stood at all sides of the corral—ten men gesticulating, leaping aloft, shouting wildly, "The whip! The whip!'

Then the Pilot stopped himself with a thrust of the fore-hoofs that buried them fetlock deep in the soil. He began to spin in the opposite direction, and Shawn's brain crumbled. He fought against defeat, but his muscles seemed to have turned numb and limp. He was leaning far to the left. Somehow he could not pull himself back into the saddle. Neither could his knees get a more secure hold, but began to loosen.

If only he could hang on for ten seconds longer . . .

Ten eternities, as soon! All at once he lost the right stirrup. He felt his right leg crawling up the flank of the spinning horse, and then all at once he was cast free and shot into the dust at the feet of Jose!

11

THERE WAS NO question of scrambling or crawling out of the danger of another of the stallion's charges. Where the outlaw fell, there he lay inert, in a crumpled heap, thoroughly stunned. It was the merest fortune that he had dropped at the feet of the Mexican, and the stallion whirled away from the threatening rope in the hand of his master.

Afterwards, Terence Shawn got uncertainly to his knees and wavered there like a pugilist trying to recover from a knockout blow and continue the fight. Continue he could not; he was beaten!

When he stood up, all at sea, he managed to maintain himself by clinging fast up the tall fence until his eyes cleared a little, and then he saw Jose leading the stallion past him and into the shack.

In time, he could follow. He sat down shakily near the door. All his leg muscles were trembling and twitching, turned quite to pulp, and he had to use will power to keep his head erect; it would have lopped over to one side like a cut branch of a tree.

Then Jose sat beside him, smoking.

"It was a bad fall, señor. However, you have no broken bones, and I shall tell you this one thing—no other man has sat the saddle on him so long as you! I thought for one moment that he had a master! Ah—well!"

There seemed a profound sorrow in his voice as he spoke.

And then he added slowly, "If you have failed, señor, who is there ever to ride him? The devil must live without a master!'

"Amigo mío," said the outlaw, beginning to roll a smoke with automatic fingers, "tell me why you hate this horse so much?"

Jose laughed savagely.

"He is a strong horse, señor, is he not?"

"He's a lion, Jose."

"He is a beautiful horse, señor?"

"He is! I have never seen a finer."

"Nor one half so fine! I, to be sure, have lived with good horses all the days of my life. I have raised them and worked them. I have exercised the thoroughbreds since I was big enough to sit in the saddle. And I never saw one before like him!"

"Then you should be happy. He's your horse."

"Tell me, señor!"

"Yes, Jose?"

"Suppose that was the best horse in the world—"

"I understand."

"Would he take the place of a son?"

"Of course not."

"Of a daughter, then?"

"Certainly he would not, Jose."

"But what of a wife, señor? You hesitate. Let me tell you. I don't mean some fat squaw that looks like a barrel with head and feet stuck onto it, but a pretty young woman with white teeth and big dark eyes. Is the horse worth a wife like that?"

"No, no, Jose. I don't have to stop to think in order to give you an answer."

"But then there are other things. A good house—a home, señor, with a pretty garden in front of it like an Americano. Vegetables behind. Some good ground. Enough for the plow, and enough for the pasture land, also. Some good cows and goats as fine as ever filled a milk can or turned on a spit. Plenty of trees for wood and for shade. A stream running around the corner of the hill, all filled with trout.

And over the mountains, deer and all that a man could care to follow with a dog and a gun. Moreover, plenty of other land to get when one wished, and get cheap. Tell me, señor, would that horse be worth such a place?'

"Well," said Terry Shawn frankly, "it depends. To a fellow who wanted a home— no. To a fellow like me, who needed wings, well—that was different!"

"Wings! Wings!" said the Mexican, suddenly hoarse with emotion. "Ah, that's the thing! But consider also that there was a position to be given up. Many kind friends. An employer out of whose pockets money ran like water out of a spring. 'How is it with you today, Jose?' 'Alas, señor, I am troubled. My wife sits at home crying for a new dress of silk, and I am a poor man.' 'Well, Jose, send her up to see the Senora. She has some things she won't wear again.' Or another time: 'It is a bright morning, Jose.' 'Yes, señor, bright for those who have sunshine in their hearts already!' 'Now what is wrong?' 'My corn is ready to reap. The wind is shaking the grain out of the heads! All will be lost!' 'Then go at once to save it. Take Miguel and Pedro and Gonzales and Federigo. Go at once, Jose! Save your corn. Take two days or three. Then come again. Ha!'

"In that manner he would speak," mused Jose bitterly. "Ah God, ah God!"

He dropped his head far down between his shoulders and was silent. Terry Shawn was silent, also. For his own part, he never could have given way to such violent emotion, but he was determined that he would not interrupt the Mexican's narrative. Here were more words than one expected from the sullen fellow, but that dual effort to ride the stallion seemed to have warmed his heart and loosened his tongue. The moment of confession was upon him, and presently he continued.

"All the way of life stretched out like a sweet road, señor. A beautiful road that goes neither high nor low, but dips pleasantly into the cool of the trees, and curves beside a river, and pauses on a hill. Children, a kind master, a good wife, a bright house, rich land, plenty of money. But then—then—"

He caught his breath and threw up both his hands in a wild gesture:

"Wings! Wings!

"One day I saw a yearling come in from the higher pastures. The whole herd gal-

91

loped; the yearling slipped out before them with his mane standing and his tail streaming behind as though it were painted on the wind. He turned his lovely head and looked back to the herd, saying, 'Let us go faster! Why do you stay behind!'

"I, Jose, beheld this. I looked at him no more. I looked up. I could not think. I went blindly home. I sat in the darkness. My wife brought me food. I thrust her away. She sent my two children. I shouted and sent them flying. All night I sat with my thoughts, and what they were you have said: Wings! Wings!

"I felt like a kitchen fowl in the yard. Feathers to beat and flutter, but they would not bear me up. But on the back of such a horse!

"Well, then, in the morning, I was already an old man. I had forgotten how to smile, for the fire was in my heart, and I walked about with my eyes turned upon the ground.

"For a year I nourished that colt. He had oats each day. He began to feel himself. He was like a stallion of four years. He scorned the earth when he walked upon it; the sound of his neigh was louder than ten horns blowing together; and his gallop was like the gliding of light over the waters.

"Now I had envy and desire in my heart, but still I was true to my master until a black day came. He had a great friend who came from Mexico City to see the rancheria and the horses. He knew horseflesh. Therefore he glanced at all the others, but when he came to the red chestnut, there he stopped.

"On the way in from the pasture I heard him talking money, and my heart stopped!

"Well, señor, I must save words and pain by telling you quickly that the next day we knew the chestnut was to go, and that night he was to leave us. When I heard that, I went down to the village church and prayed for strength, but no strength came to me, and in the middle of the night I went into the stable and brought out the colt.

"I did not even think to take one of my own horses to ride. I never had committed any crime before. Only this one! And I said to myself that if I took this one horse, at least I left behind me my wife, my two children, my house, my lands and all my old hopes in life. Pile all of them into the scales; weigh them against the horse and

93

you yourself have said what is the difference.

"Well, señor, I understand that the lawyers would not have understood what I
meant, but I felt that God would understand, and the tender Virgin. So I went
out from my old life with empty hands and
only that colt. There was a halter and a
rope, and my feet and hands. That was
how I began again.

"I went for the high mountains; they pursued me; I escaped from them. I ran like
a deer, and the colt ran beside me. For
ten days they hunted us, and the ribs began
to stand out through the skin of the chestnut, but at last we escaped. Then for two
years I wandered. All men knew what I
had done and all men were against me;
therefore what do I do? I steal, I rob, and
I hunt not animals but men.

"At last every trail is on fire against me
and I cross the river to the northern shore.
I am an exile and my only companion is
my horse. And still, señor, I am on foot!
Why? Because evil has come into the soul
of the colt. A petted child is the son of
the devil. A petted horse is a spoiled horse.
Besides, I had no chance to break him
properly, for where I paused was only for

the day or the night. Then I must march on again.

"A hundred times I tried to ride him; he learned to pitch me from the saddle as he pitched you this night! At length I made my heart hard, for I was in a torture, having given up my life for the sake of a horse which was a curse to me. I determined that I would conquer him by time and cruelty, and therefore I made up my mind to what?"

"To starve him?" suggested Shawn curiously.

"Yes, señor! But you shall hear!"

12

THE MEXICAN'S EXCITEMENT had been growing for some time, and now it became so great that his voice trembled and his words stumbled upon one another.

"I began to see," he explained, in his growing hysteria. "I began to understand that it was no horse but a devil. A devil it had been in the first place that tempted me away from my happy life, my home, my work, and gave me that madman's desire for wings that would carry me faster than any pursuit could follow, make me strong enough to strike down my enemies and escape from their vengeance, make me free in spite of numbers. So the Lord was tempted by Satan. So poor Jose was tempted by a devil looking at me out of the eyes of a horse. When I began to see this, then I swore that I would conquer him or kill him, or he should kill me!

"I starved him, then, until he was so weak that I could mount him and he could not buck me off. Then I made him go forward. I was cruel. I think that I should have mastered him if it had not been that the devil intervened again. That day he brought on my trail three old enemies from south of the Rio Grande, and they rushed after me.

"There was nothing for me to do but to hurry ahead. That horse which was too weak to pitch me from the saddle still could gallop a little, and as long as he could stagger, his stagger was faster than the running of their horses.

At last they persisted no longer. For two days they had followed me, and for two days I had tortured the chestnut; then I dismounted and saw that he was no better than a dead horse. He would take neither food nor water and only had strength to brace his legs for a few moments before he dropped down. So I left him and carried the saddle back through the trees.

"See, then, that the devil was not through with me, but wished to ruin me completely with this horse. That dying horse he put in the wise hands of Señor Shawn, who brought him back to life once more, and from Señor Shawn the horse was given to another, and from the other I claimed my property. And so here he is again. Once more I may talk with him. Once more he can tempt me and damn me. Señor, I have opened my heart. Now tell me why it is that I cannot raise a rifle and put a bullet through his head?"

He had shouted out the last words, throwing up his hands and beating them back against his face and his breast; his voice broke almost into a sob of desperation.

Shawn had listened to this story in the greatest amazement. Now he said, "You steady down, Jose. Let me tell you that you're wrong about one thing. I didn't gentle the stallion. All I know, I'll tell you. I came through the mountains with twenty men behind me and a dying horse under me. I hit a little valley on the face of Mount Shannon, and there I met an oldish sort of a fellow, deaf and dumb, living like a hermit. He had that chestnut before his shack, and I roped and saddled it and left some money for boot and then rode like the devil.

"I made all the distance from Mount Shannon down through Overbury Cañon and then out to Clinker and back near Lister. I left the poor old sheriff damning his heart and his horses clean out of sight and distance, and then I kept on, and the chestnut never said no. Still, Jose, I didn't know what a treasure he was, and so I swapped him in simply because he was tired at last. If I'd known—he never would have come back to you, Jose!"

"You are not a believer," answered Jose sternly. "You cannot see that men have nothing to do with this, and the spirits have everything. Only, señor, you have not explained one thing. How did you ride my horse down from the mountains? No other man ever dared to sit on his back!"

"I'll be honest, Jose. I rode him just as I found him. He never looked worn once on the way. He never so much as shied, and he never said no to me, no matter what I asked of him. He went all day, and he was coming up against the bit when I finally got rid of him. That's all I know, Jose."

"The hand of God! The hand of God!" said Jose.

"The hand of the old hermit up on Mount Shannon," answered the outlaw. "If there's a mystery, it's in how that old tenderfoot managed to take that dying horse you talk about and turn him into what we see inside the house, here."

"It is true. That is very strange," murmured the Mexican, his thoughts turning in a strong river in this new direction. "Deaf and dumb, did you say?"

"Yes."

Jose nodded. Then he continued, "That is a sign also. God is upon that man with a curse or with a blessing. All who come into the life of the chestnut are marked men."

"With the hoofs or otherwise," grinned Shawn. He stood up.

"How long do you stay here, Jose?"

"How can I tell?" answered Jose in a wild and gloomy voice. "I am clay, and God or the devil molds me. I stay here until a voice comes, and I know that I shall hear one."

He said it with the strong reasonableness

with which an unbalanced man pronounces his favorite doctrine.

"Wait only a few days," said the outlaw. "I'm coming back again. I'll ride the Pilot, or he'll ride me. Adios, Jose!" There was no answer from Jose.

He had seated himself in the doorway of the shack and fallen into a brown study; so the outlaw moved away and went back to his horse, which he found grazing contentedly on the steep bank of the stream. It tossed its head and pricked its ears to welcome its rider. So Shawn mounted, and as he walked the horse away, he heard again the jangling of a guitar made soft in the distance, and faintly he could make out the singing of Jose.

He told himself that surely the Mexican was mad, but nevertheless that explanation did not entirely satisfy him. He had his own share of superstitions picked up along the range, and the solemn narrative of Jose had turned his blood a little cold.

In the meantime, however, he told himself that he had something even more important than the discharge of his debt to Shannon, or the acquisition of Sky Pilot— and that was the meeting with the girl the following morning.

It was late, now. His bones were growing sore from the heavy falls which he had received; therefore he turned aside into the woods, and in the first convenient little clearing he made a soft bed of pine boughs and rolled himself in his blanket.

He could not sleep at once, however, but lay on his back listening to the crunching jaws of the horse as it grazed on the long, rich grass, and to the whisperings and sighings of the wind through the trees. Now and again a breeze of added force touched one of the pines, and far away or near a bough rubbed against another with a mournful groaning sound. Above him, the stars shone white and still; he looked up through the strange spaces and through the dark and empty holes where no stars at all were shining, and the mind of Terence Shawn began to grapple with new ideas that troubled him—with thoughts of old Shannon on the mountain, the madman, Jose, and Kitty Bowen, last of all, and not less wonderful to him than the brightest of those stars in the sky.

At last, he turned upon his face to shut out these disturbing ideas, and he fell into a sound sleep.

When he wakened, it was the first of the dawn.

A thin fog had risen during the night. His face and hands were wet, the blanket was damp, and all the trees were dripping softly in the silver gloom. The horse, having found a thick bed of pine needles, still lay asleep, with prone head, and its breath rose in white puffs that melted instantly into the fog.

When he sat up, his bones ached sadly from his falls of the preceding evening; this world seemed a gloomy place and hard to understand, but at least the mysteries of the Mexican's belief now appeared merest moonshine and nonsense. It was a wake-aday world once more, made up of men, women, horses, guns, and similar hard and substantial facts. As for that realm of spirits which obtruded itself upon the Mexican, it was the fancy of a madman!

So thought Terence Shawn, and mechanically went about the building of a fire and the preparation of his breakfast. Food was tasteless, however. For with a growing excitement he looked forward to the possible meeting with the girl. He began, like all who are truly hopeful of great happiness, to discount what she had promised for certainly girls make promises easily and break them with equal fluency; so he told himself that there was hardly a chance in ten.

The evening before, she had been excited to see him at the dance, defying all the powers of the law so blandly. But now it would be very different, and when she wakened and saw the world turned gray with this disheartening mist, she would forget the night before.

After his morning meal, he looked over his horse with his usual care. The work of the day before had been very exacting, but, nevertheless, the horse had stood up under it well, and with a kind eye it sniffed at the bridle and saddle which its master brought toward it. Upon that important point, therefore, he was reassured, and he swung into the damp saddle, at the last, certain that if danger came near, he could come close to showing it a clean pair of heels, on that day.

He took his bearings, after that, as nicely as he was able. The fog had not lifted. The weird, pale mist still tangled in the woods and breathed cloudily down the draws, but at length he had located himself, and he took his way toward that cañon leading out from Lister where he had promised that he would meet the girl.

It was well after eight when he entered the cañon. He cursed the haste that had brought him there so much before the time; for it is better to arrive almost exactly on time, of course. This long delay would try all his nerves with expectancy!

He barely had made up his mind to that fact when, as he galloped on, he made out the dim, dim outline of a rider just before him, traveling up the valley. He checked his horse to a trot and stole closer, and suddenly he knew that it was no man but a woman who was showing him the way up the cañon.

13

IT WAS KITTY BOWEN.

She turned her horse when she heard him and came smiling through the mist.

"How did you guess," asked Kitty, "that I'd be an hour early?"

"I didn't," he confessed. "I didn't guess that you'd come at all. But I'm terrible glad that you did."

"I had to tell them that I was starting

for town to see Jenny Moran," she said. "And of course I had to start early. They suspect me, you know; they watch me every minute, now!"

"They watch you?" repeated the outlaw. "And who are they?"

She paused a moment and watched his lean and handsome face hardening and the keen narrowing of his eyes; so that a little tremor ran through the girl.

"Since you danced with me," said Kitty Bowen, "they think that you may come to see me again. They think that I may be the bait, Terry, with which they'll catch the fish!"

"It's the sheriff?" asked Shawn.

"Of course."

"It's a low thing to do," observed Shawn bitterly. "And what do your mother and father say?"

"They're worried, too," she answered frankly.

"Ay," said Shawn. "They wouldn't be having you run about with a man like me— a robber, Kitty, and a murderer, and a man of no faith. They've told you that, I've no doubt?"

"Well," said Kitty, "how good are you, Terry, and how bad?"

She added, "We'd better be drifting up the cañon; I think the sun's coming out, Terry.

They turned their horses up the ravine, accordingly, and, glancing to the east, Shawn saw that the pale disk of the sun was looking more and more brightly through the fog, making one quarter of the heavens a glowing, translucent, pearly white. Still the mist did not clear, and the black, wet trees dripped mournfully beside them, or over them, as they went up the narrowing ravine. It seemed to Shawn that he could not have chosen a more unlucky moment to see the girl. In a time of bright sun and a cool wind, say, the life of an outlawed man might seem joyful enough in the wilderness; but now his existence must appear to the girl very like that of a drowned rat.

"That's a hard thing to be asking a man," said Terry. "You better ask the others. I'd rather."

"I've asked both kinds," said she.

"What kinds?"

"Those that hate you and those that love you."

"Those that love me?" exclaimed Shawn.

"Old Joe, for instance," said the girl, smiling a little.

"Him?" cried Terry Shawn. "I've never had a good word out of him in my life long! Nothing but hard cracks and meanness, confound him! He was joking with you, if he said a good word about me, Kitty"

In place of answering, she looked straight up the valley and smiled a little.

"According to Joe," she filled in at last, "you're a saint and a prince without a princedom, Terry. You've never done any wrong to anyone, except when you've been forced against the wall, a few times.

"Humph!" said he.

"The reason you're poor is that you give your money away. The reason that you have to keep running is that you've taken money from one man to give it to another. And, after all, Terry, you *aren't* very rich, I suppose!"

He was silent.

It began to appear to Shawn that this girl was bantering him mercilessly, making rather a fool of him. For all the while as she spoke, she turned a faint smile upon him, whether a smile of the lips or of the eyes. Indeed, she impressed him rather like a keen-minded man than as a woman. He was thrust away at arm's length, and he felt a bit of nervousness mastering him.

"Then," she continued, as he remained silent and stared at the wet rocks over which they were passing, "there are the others. They say the opposite things."

"The sheriff?"

"Yes, and most of the rest."

"Opposite things such as what?"

"That you're a thief."

"Ah," murmured Shawn.

"A bank breaker."

He flinched.

"A horse stealer."

"I've paid double for every horse I ever took!" he cried.

"After taking them by force," she answered, looking so straight at him that his head dropped again.

"And," she went on, "they tell me that you're a remorseless enemy, and that you never forgive an evil turn."

"I don't know," muttered Shawn. "An eye for an eye—"

"That's Old Testament," she answered. "But they say that you've killed men—that you always will keep on killing them—that you like to kill—that you're a murderer!"

Now, as she brought out this indictment, he began to speak in answer at each pause, but when she had concluded he was sitting stiff in the saddle, pale, lips pressed hard together, perspiration beaded on his forehead.

"Is it true?" she asked him.

He tried to answer. He found his voice and shouted, "No, no, no, by God! It's a lie!"

It was as though he were shouting the words for the whole world to hear, but the girl tilted her head to one side, and still he thought that there was a faint smile in her eyes as she listened.

"I've never fired at any man," he said, "except when I was cornered, except—except—"

He paused and looked at her desperately.

"I could understand a lot," she said, with a sudden warmth. "You go ahead and talk it right out to me, Terry, just as if I were a man."

So saying, she let her horse drift a little closer to him.

"Well, God bless you," said Shawn. "You're the right stuff. Only, it's hard to know where to begin. About the thieving—suppose that we begin there—"

"Begin at the end and not at the beginning," she suggested. "I know, somehow, that you never took from a poor fellow who couldn't afford a loss. And I've heard—well, about the Bunyan bank—how you sent back half of what you took, when you heard that they were having to close down because of the loss. Ah, but it isn't that. Of course it's bad—but somehow it doesn't bother me much, and I suppose you did it more for the fun than for the money. However, the other thing is different, isn't it? How many men actually—have you killed, Terry?"

He counted them up slowly in his mind.

"Sloan," he said, "Justis, Morgental, Devine, Ross, Perkins, and Chicago Jim."

He made a pause between each name.

"That's seven," she said cheerfully.

"That's seven," he said, and he moistened his dry lips and looked askance to her for judgment.

"But there are all sorts of people," said the girl, nodding and frowning. "Even Dad says that there are some men who need killing."

He reined his horse closer. "I'll tell you, Kitty. You take Sloan. He was a bully from the mines. I was only a kid. Sloan tried to bully me at the Dickins Bar in Phoenix. You know, Kitty, I was afraid. I'd never pulled a gun on anything but rabbits. I had to fight or show yellow. I—well, I killed him, Kitty, you see.

She nodded.

"Justis was a toplofty Englishman and a scoundrel; he tried to run off with my sister. No marriage or nothing, Kitty. When I stopped him, he tried to shoot me down, but he was just a mite slow. Then there was Morgental, the gambler. A crook and a snake. He tried to shoot me from behind. There's the scar across the back of my neck. But as I fell, I twisted over backwards and shot him over my shoulder, you see."

Her interruption seemed to him perfectly without reason or sense.

"How old were you then, Terry?"

"Then? Oh, eighteen, I suppose. And then—"

"That was three at eighteen," said Kitty.

"You see that it wasn't my fault those three times?"

"Of course I see that."

"Devine was a hired man. He came down from Montana with five hundred dollars in his pocket and another thousand promised if he managed to get me. Well, he missed, and I spent the five hundred on his funeral, which was the only fair thing to do. There was Ross and Perkins. Ross came after me because I'd killed Devine. He caught up with me in the Sierras near the edge of a little town and we had it out. Hand to hand. He didn't die for a week. Perkins was a great pal of Ross. He took my trail because I'd killed him. Two years later we met. It was a fair fight and a fair draw. He had me through the hip and the stomach. He was fast as lightning, but my shot hit him between the eyes. I was six months getting on my feet."

Kitty had turned very white.

"Chicago Jim was the last. There wasn't any cause. There was nothing between us, but he wanted to get a reputation. He was a game one, and I wanted to nail him through the hip only, but I slipped and it hit him in the body. Well, that makes seven, Kitty."

"Only seven?" said Kitty, with an odd smile. "Only seven, Terry?"

He rubbed his hard knuckles across his chin.

"I wasn't counting Mexicans," said Terry.

14

HE FELT, AS he said it, that something was wrong—that it would have been very well for him, if he could have avoided that last statement. Kitty Bowen looked downwards at the ground for a time, thoughtful and still.

Then she drew her horse to a halt.

They had come to the sharp turn in the ravine, where it spread out in a broader and more level floor before them, not over-shadowed with such lofty trees, but rather broken, here and there, with tufts and patches of foliage. The wind came up this more open valley and bore in its arms rapid and thick drifts of the fog which had been growing more and more translucent, sometimes like glowing pearl; sometimes the fog was blown toward them like white fire.

Now the damp wind made Kitty's face shine, and the wisps of her curling hair were printed close against her pink cheeks, so that she became a very wet beauty indeed as she sat there before the outlaw, kneading her reins with one nervous hand, and with the other tapping the butt of her riding whip on the pommel of her saddle.

She looked straight at Mr. Shawn, and he wished that she were looking almost any other place in the world.

"I'd like to know!" said Kitty.

"Well?" murmured Terry Shawn.

"How many Mexicans were there, Terry? They're human beings, aren't they?"

"I live the way that I see a chance to live," he insisted. "But if I seen a chance to do better—I mean, if I had something else to live for—"

"I didn't come out here to talk like that," said Kitty. "I've got to go back." She turned the head of her horse.

"Damnation!" exclaimed Mr. Shawn, and with a prick of the spurs, he lifted his horse fairly across her way.

Kitty turned white. For, indeed, no one in the world could have been prepared for the sudden change that had occurred in the outlaw. It was like seeing a sword in a showcase, one moment, and the next held level with one's eyes by the hand of a skilled enemy.

She knew that she was safe, of course.

In the West there are certain laws, even for outlaws. And yet for one dreadful moment she could not be sure.

"You knew, too," said Terence Shawn in a ringing voice. "Of course you knew that I was crazy about you when I went into the dance hall last night because I couldn't keep away. You knew when you came out this morning that I'd tell you that I loved you, but you just thought that you'd try the high hand and keep me under. I tell you, you can't. You can have done with me, mighty quick. Say the word and I'll never cross your trail again. But if you want to think me over—here I am and here I'll always be. My God, Kitty, I'd peel off all my skin and wear a new color for you. I'd work harder than a beaver for you. I'd build you a house and work in the ground for you. I'd make you happy or die trying. You knew I was a gun fighter before ever you let me meet you here. Now you know some more facts. Do you want to hear something extra?"

As this torrent of words burst upon Kitty's ears, the last vestige of her calm smile, her easy superiority in this bold situation, was stripped from her. She shrank smaller in her saddle. She watched him,

115

fascinated, and the yes that fell from her lips was spoken automatically.

"I'll tell you, then, I've never gone after a clean, decent fellow, and the skunks that I've accounted for, I'm glad of. And I love the fighting. I'd rather have a good fight than a million dollars. I like the snarl on the mouth of the other fellow, and the second of quiet before the draw, when his nerves are working on him and he has to go first for his gun. I love it, you see? Only, I love one thing better, and that's you. D'you hear? I'd chuck it all for you, quit clean, turn around and start new, and once I made the new start, I'd never go back on you. Have you got anything to say?"

"I have to go home," said Kitty weakly.

"Have you got anything to say?" he repeated savagely.

And, pressing his horse closer, an arm and hand of iron passed around Kitty. She was trembling so violently that she could not manage to free herself; her wits were quite dissolved and no words would come to her.

15

Now Kitty Bowen, as she drew back toward her home, found the thought of a ride into Lister a great bore. She wanted at once to be alone among familiar objects, and, above all, she wanted to be alone in her own room.

So she cast discretion to the winds and turned back into the ranch house, when she said goodbye to Terry Shawn.

So she came home, unsaddled her horse, turned it into the corral, tossed a pitchfork load of hay over the fence for it, and went into the house. On the side veranda she came straight upon the sheriff and could not help starting back with an exclamation.

The sheriff did not rise. He maintained his position in the chair, slumped far down on the middle of his spine. Only, at sight of her, he began to waggle the upper one of his crossed legs more violently, like a golfer addressing a difficult shot.

"Hullo, an' how are you, Kitty?" asked the sheriff. "And what the devil kind of mischief have you been into now?"

"What a queer thing to ask!" said Kitty,

frowning. This morning, she did not like this badinage, and the sheriff suddenly appeared to her an unkempt, irritating, slovenly, wrinkled, ridiculous, and terrible person. She had to bite her lip to prevent that opinion from shining forth from her face. The sheriff, however, appeared oblivious of the bad impression he was making.

"You wouldn't talk up to me about it," he nodded. "But I can guess, honey, I can guess. Dancin' around with gunmen in the night, and—"

He was shaking a long forefinger at her in amused anger; but Kitty flushed and rushed suddenly past him into the house.

At this, he shrank still lower into his chair, his great, spindling shanks stretched awkwardly before him. Clothes never were made to fit the sheriff accurately, and long before he had given up the effort to find a tidy measure.

He was a caricature; he knew it and almost had forgotten to be hurt by the smiles which greeted him on all sides. Yet, in a way, he knew that his popularity was founded in a large measure upon his absurd appearance; for instance, who could be jealous of the gun fighting and brave exploits of a man who, in all other respects, was totally absurd? So the votes always were cast for Lank Heney, and he remained sheriff indefinitely, smiled at, scoffed at, shrugged at, but trusted by all of the law-abiding people of the range and dreaded equally by the criminals. And the sheriff had almost forgotten, in the process of time, that his skin was very thin indeed, that shame and misery were as wife and child to him, and that nothing remained for him in life except to exist as a sort of ridiculous hero.

He had forgotten these things until the girl rushed past him with scorn and anger and disappeared into the house.

A door clicked, and the sheriff rose slowly from the chair, unlimbered his awkward height with a yawn and stretch or two, and then walked with a slouching stride down the veranda, down the steps, and away.

He did not take his horse; in fact, he intended only to stroll aimlessly up and down for a short time until the pain in his breast had subsided a little. He followed the fresh sign of the horse on which Kitty had ridden back to the house. Just beside it, and weaving now and again across the second trail, was the sign of her going forth, and the active eye of the sheriff noted the differences. Little pebbles, dust grains were still dislodging from the upper edges and the sides of the latter set of tracks and rolling down into the pits of the hoofprints. But the earlier prints, though hardly much more than an hour old, already were settled. Both sets had been made within the last two or three hours, because the fog and misting rain had not yet wet down the tracks nor drenched the cracks where the dry underearth showed through.

He regarded these things with a careless and yet an occupied eye, and presently he turned off from the straight path away from the house and found himself following the trail toward the nearest copse; certainly she had told the truth and had been riding up the valley, and not down it! In the meantime, it eased the sheriff to have this foolishly small employment. He had come out to the Bowen house on request, to use the place as headquarters in the hunt for the great outlaw, Shawn; and this little encounter with the girl had crossed him like a sudden and blighting shadow.

He advanced, then, toward the trees, following the trail with a mere touch of the eyes, now and then, and so, as he came close to the edge of the woodland, he noticed another set of hoofmarks in the grass. Here they came to a pause, turned back, entered the trees. Here they passed straight on down the valley toward Lister. Here the tracks of the girl's horse had turned to the side—and here the other rider had come alongside.

What manner of horse had made those tracks, then? Or might it not be that the second trail had been made at a different time?

Upon his knees, almost prayerfully, the sheriff hoped so, but he saw that he was wrong. Just as the grass was reerecting itself in one set of hoof hollows, so it was rising once more in the other. And the look of the gravel in one shallow hole was like the look in the next.

No, those two had ridden side by side— unless it were that the second rider had trailed the first.

No, that was not possible, either, for the hoofs of the girl's horse had remained on the narrow bridle path, and the other rider had taken the rough on one side or the other as a man, say, would do to please a lady . . .

Who, then, could be afraid to come to Bowen's place? One under the shadow of the law—such a one as handsome, young Terence Shawn who, the very night before, had dared to enter the dance hall in the town of Lister and, while there, had made an eminent fool of Sheriff Lank Heney.

16

NOW SHERIFF HENEY became at once the man of action.

He cut straight through the rear of the woods to the back of the Bowen place, where he caught up his mustang, whipped and spurred the antics and pitching out of the system of that tough-mouthed little mongrel, and then raced him back to the valley trail.

As he shot past the house, he saw Kitty's face at a window, and he couldn't tell whether the face was pale through fear or only seemed blurred to paleness by the speed of his going, but in his heart of hearts he shrewdly suspected that the girl guessed at his mission. He wished, then, that he had departed more secretly, but there was such a fire burning in the soul of the sheriff that it drove him recklessly on until he actually came to the woods in the ravine.

There he checked his pace a little—not to an easy trot or canter, but to a gallop at which he still could sweep and probe the trees before him with some degree of thoroughness. He sustained that pace for a considerable distance, and then he saw suddenly what he wanted—not glimpsed far away, but startlingly close.

He was riding in a little woodland lane, the floor compacted and deadened by a thick packing of pine needles which deadened the sound of his hoofbeats; so, looking to the left, the sheriff saw another horseman riding down just such another winding lane, and not twenty yards distant. They looked at one another in the same instant; he recognized Terry Shawn and reached for his gun, and he saw Shawn grab at his own weapon.

There was this difference between them, that the sheriff, as he sighted the foe, steadied his horse and called to stop it, so that his marksmanship might be a little more accurate, whereas Shawn, with a shout and a touch of his knee, turned his mount straight through the trees. He was charging the enemy as he fired!

Never had Lank Heney been so keen as he was on this day; never had his hand been so swift; and the result was that he got in the first shot, firing from the hip. He knew that shot was low to the right; his second was equally high to the left; but before he could get in a third bullet that would split the difference between the other two and drop Terry Shawn from the saddle, the latter, charging fiercely, had fired in turn.

Kind Providence in a measure saved the sheriff. His mustang, stopping short, swerved a little to the side and, squatting on its hind legs, threw up its head. Straight through that head went the bullet from the outlaw's gun, and the little mustang pitched on its side, dead.

Not all the activity of the long-legged sheriff could avoid that fall. He barely managed to shake his feet loose from the stirrups; then he was sent spinning, head over heels. His head struck a root. He came up staggering, dizzy, his hand empty of its Colt, and found Terry Shawn just before him, with a gun tipped lightly in his fingers, ready to drop it on the mark.

"Hello," said Shawn. "I see you're a popular sort of a man, Lank."

The sheriff said nothing, but blinked his way back to full consciousness.

"Even your horse will die for you," explained the outlaw with a grin. "What sent you zooming down the valley on my trail this morning, sheriff?"

Lank regarded him with a quiet interest; his time to die had come, and he was amazed that his approaching end troubled him so little.

"A touch of luck," said the sheriff. "And a touch of luck beat me."

"We'll call it luck," nodded Shawn with much good nature, "after you've missed two shots! Now, what'll I do with you, Lank?"

"Don't it look like a good place for a shooting?" inquired the sheriff.

"What am I to do?" answered the other. "Drop you in cold blood?"

"You'd hang back on account of that, I suppose," answered Lank Heney dryly.

Mr. Shawn grew pink.

"I'm a skunk, then, it seems," he said.

The sheriff regarded him with bright, cold, hostile eyes. Being about to die, he was frank.

"You are," said he.

"And that's why you've been hunting me so extra hard?"

"To get you out of the way," declared

Lank Heney, "I would of given a leg or an arm—my right arm."

"How did I ever harm you?" asked the younger man, canting his head curiously to one side.

"How did you ever harm me?" echoed the sheriff. "Ain't you been hell-raising in this county time out of mind?"

"I never took a penny from your pocket."

"You been defyin' the law," said the sheriff.

"You never made those laws; what's the damn law to you?" asked the boy.

"What it is to everybody," answered Lank Heney. "The law's what gives every kid a chance to grow into a man, and every man a chance to keep what he makes. What's the law to me? Why, kid, the law's my uncle and father and brother, the same as it is to everybody except the poison-hearted wolves like you! And it's the law that'll get you, Shawn, and hang you up with a rope and watch you kicking!"

"Thanks," said Terence Shawn. "Damned if I don't think that you mean what you say. But look here, Lank—who made you the grandpa of the law, this way? You ain't making' an election speech, now, you know!"

The sheriff flushed.

"I never made an election speech in my life," said he. "For the rest of it, you're a murderin' thief, Shawn. Drop your gun and finish me. I'm done talkin' to you!"

"Turn your face to that tree," said Terence Shawn.

"I'll see you damned first," said Lank Heney. "I'll take mine in front."

"All right," said the boy. "You're a nervy fellow, sheriff. Maybe I could take some sort of a message for you to your folks."

"I got no folks," said Lank.

"Not even a cousin?"

"Not even a cousin.

"Well, then, you'd want to remember some friend?"

"I got no friend," said the homely sheriff.

"No folks—no friend?" said the outlaw. "Nobody to leave your guns to?"

The sheriff scratched his chin.

"I would sort of like," said he, "that my guns might be nailed up in the sheriff's office in Lister and that it might be wrote under them that dying didn't bother me none."

Mr. Shawn narrowed his keen eyes and waited for a moment.

"You ain't going to break me down," shouted the sheriff angrily. "But go ahead and finish, will you?"

"I got an idea," said the outlaw in a curious voice, "that you're one of the kind of folks that I used to read about in school. One of them that are sorry that they only got one life to lay down for their country."

"You're a skunk, Shawn," said the sheriff fiercely. "But what you say don't bother me none."

"You start thinkin' on this," said the outlaw. "When you're dead and rotten, nobody'll ever think twice about what you were or what you done. You got no family; you got no friends; you got nothing to grieve for you or remember you, sheriff!"

"I don't need none," cried poor Lank Heney desperately. "I know that I've done my duty and rode hard and played fair, and worked for the law. I've done my job the best that I could—and God have mercy on my soul. Shoot and be damned, Shawn!"

Terence Shawn began to rein back his horse.

"I'll take you at long range," said he. "The trouble with you, sheriff, was that you never learned how to shoot. If you was to get another chance at life, you'd better settle down and practice a couple of hours a day. Your first shot missed my knee and your second one shaved my right ear, and I wasn't twenty yards away. That's pretty careless shooting, sheriff, even if it was a moving target. You might do for a barroom fight, Lank, but out in the open with a Colt you ain't much good. You should of stuck to a Winchester. Slower but surer. I tell you what, Lank, don't you go around tryin' to look like a hare when God meant you to be a tortoise. Slow and sure had ought to of been your motto. Steady now—"

The sheriff made a single step forward and raised himself to his full height. He saw the glimmer of light on the short barrel of the revolver; a steady, shining streak that would let immortality into his soul. Then he closed his eyes and let the sweet face of Kitty Bowen blossom in his imagination.

He steadied himself, his nerves as taut as strings of a violin. There was no shot. Then a fury seized the sheriff. This man was playing with him, taunting and scorning him, and waiting for his strength of will to break down.

"You damn, yellow-hearted scoundrel!" cried the sheriff.

And he opened his eyes.

He looked around him then and he saw with utter amazement that there was no rider before him, and no threatening revolver leveled. He stared wildly, but he saw that he was alone in the woods.

Then, out of the distance, he thought that he heard laughter. He dropped on one knee and listened, and he made out with certainty the soft pounding of departing hoofs.

After that, he stood up slowly. His head was whirling. In his heart there was a fixed and unshakable element of piety, but now the sheriff could not make out whether God or Terence Shawn was to be thanked for the life which had not been taken from him on this day.

17

THERE WAS A day to be killed, and the first part of it the outlaw spent in drifting slowly across country until he came to the shack of his friend, Joe. That amiable and shiftless puncher should have been at work riding herd on his small band of cattle, for they needed his attention. Instead, Mr. Shawn looked in upon him when the man was employed in his shack in the important labor of garnishing a saddle with some intricate carved designs.

When the shadow of Shawn fell upon him, Joe did not look up.

"Where did you learn to do that work?" said Shawn.

"Stand out of me light," said Joe. "You know little about me, kid, and what I can do. I ain't spent all my life on the range."

"It ain't a true thing they tell of you, though," suggested Shawn.

"What ain't true?" asked the artist, bending more closely over his work.

"That you were a racetrack tout down at New Orleans?"

"Will you back up and gimme air?" cried the angry artist.

"Or that you sailed before the mast," went on Shawn innocently, "and used to live on hardtack and kicks all the way around the Horn?"

"It's a lie!" yelled Joe, now looking up.

"I see that your arm's tattooed, though," said the observer. "Why did you have it done?"

"Why would you think?" asked the other dryly.

"I can't tell," said Shawn, "whether it would be so's other people could know you, or so's you could know yourself."

"You're kind of full of yourself this mornin', kid," declared Joe. "You need work, I'd say. You been stall-fed too long and nobody's been ridin' you. Now, leave that saddle alone!" For his guest was bending over the carving.

"What might this be, Joe?"

"What would you take it for?"

"A fat woman out of a circus running through fire."

"You got no eye," said Joe scornfully. "You fellows. You spend your time lookin' at cows and rocks until you don't see nothin' worth while. That's a Fiji belle doin' a dance like she done it for me."

"With that few clothes, Joe?"

"What is clothes to an artist?" asked Joe with a higher tone. "We painters and carvers, we want to get down to the facts."

"Over here," said Shawn in continuation, "is an ostrich eating a rattlesnake."

"Terry, you're a blockhead and a sap," explained Joe. "That's a lark that's found a worm."

"I never knew that larks went in so heavy on legs, Joe."

"You never knew nothing except guns and hosses."

"It's got an enlarged hock, this here lark," remarked the outlaw.

"Lemme see," said the anxious artist. "Aw, I see what you mean. Nobody but a mean-hearted buzzard like you would ever take notice of a little thing like that. Well, a man's knife will slip, once in a while."

"Over here on this side," said Shawn, "I see that you got a—"

"Never mind what I got," answered Joe hotly. "I never met the mate of you, Terry, for spoilin' things with fool talk. Shut up and get out, because I'm busy."

Instead, the outlaw sat down in a corner.

"Turn up some chuck, Joe," said he, "I'm hungry. And let's hear the news."

Joe, grumbling but obedient, fell to work rousing a fire and preparing food.

"There ain't much news," said he, "except about one man."

"Who is that?"

"The orneriest, lowest-down snake that ever bothered folks in this part of the world," answered the other.

133

"I dunno who you mean," said the outlaw.

"He come into town the other night and made eyes at pretty Kitty Bowen," said Joe. "The sheriff, he took pity on him and let him dance around with Kitty, but he expected that this here Shawn would stand and fight like a man, after the dance was ended. Instead, what would you think Shawn done? He jumped out a window and sneaked away like a low hound."

"Maybe he didn't want to spoil the dance floor," suggested Terry with a yawn.

"And now Lister is risin'," continued Joe.

"Lister is always rising," remarked Shawn, "and then settling down again. How d'you know it's rising?"

"The Patrick boys come riding by; they'd been telephoned to their house from town. It's this here Shawn had got up the back of Bowen pretty high and he's just out and offered twenty-five hundred spot cash on top of the reward."

Shawn sat up, his eyes bright and narrowed with attention.

"And why's that?" he asked.

"I dunno. It seems that Shawn has been

gallivantin' around the Bowen house. Still after Kitty! And folks are tired of Shawn. They say," explained Joe, "that they don't mind him lifting the cash out of a bank safe or holding up a train or something like that, once in a while. They don't mind dropping a thug, once in a while, because it gives the boys something to talk about when the winter nights get long and the magazines give out in the bunkhouse. But what they terrible much do mind, kid, is having you fool around with the prettiest girl in the county!"

"They want her?" asked Shawn scornfully. "Then why don't they take her?"

"D'you want her?" asked Joe suddenly.

"What if I do? Whose business is it?"

"Your business. It's your business if you want her. It's her pa's business, too.

"I dunno that I follow that."

"Her old man would be askin' what would you do with her?"

"Suppose that I was to shake the old game and turn straight for her, Joe?"

"When did you start on your own?"

"I was thirteen."

"That's ten years ago?"

135

"It is."

"How many days' work have you done in them ten years?"

"I suppose—hell, I don't know, if you come down to that," said Terry, turning sullen.

"It's what it pretty near comes down to," replied Joe. "You've floated along for ten years. Now you say that you want to turn and swim back upstream Kid, you never could even get back to where you started from."

"I hear you croaking," said Shawn in a rising temper. "But it don't mean nothing to me."

"You couldn't live without a gun in your hand," said Joe thoughtfully.

"Me? I couldn't? Joe, you don't know nothing about me. I could settle down like nothing at all and work like hell twenty hours a day for twenty years. Guns? I could leave 'em off forever. I'm tired of the weight of packing them around."

"You couldn't even sleep without a gun beside you."

"Joe, there ain't a man in the world that's got more makings of a peaceable gent than I have. Fighting? I could quit it. I will quit it. I tell you right now, I'll never pull an-

136

other gun. By God, you wait and see if I ever do!"

"Never pull another gun?"

"Never."

"Not even on a rabbit?"

"Don't be a fool. I mean on a man. No. I'll be through with all that."

"Kid, will you lemme tell you something?"

"I hear you."

"You'll never change. It's in the blood of you. It's in the bone of you. Hitch wings onto a bird and it'll fly, won't it? Same way with you. You got to have a little hellfire around you once in a while, or you'd curl up and die."

"Hell-fire? Hell-fire?" said Shawn with a growing irritation. "I dunno that I like the way that you put that, Joe."

"I put it again. You got a taste for meanness and fighting."

"Joe," said the other sternly, "you've said about enough."

"Work? The kind of work that you'd do would be the raising of calluses, reaching into the pockets of other folks."

"Joe, you're steppin' over the line!" cried Shawn.

He turned white with rage.

"You low rat," he added, "you wear a gun! Go for it before you try to talk to me like that!"

Instead of reaching for his gun, Joe relaxed in a broad smile.

"You see for yourself," said he. "You was just promising that you would never pull a gun again. In half a minute I got you right up to the murder stage. Trust you? Why, hell, kid, you can see that you can't trust yourself!"

Mr. Shawn listened and bit his lip. He turned toward the door; he turned back again.

"Joe!" he said in a broken voice.

"Leave out the rest of it," said Joe cheerfully. "Set down and rest your feet and eat something. We'll tie to some sort of an idea, out of all of this!"

But Terry Shawn sat disconsolate, his elbows on his knees, staring with great eyes at the future. It had been to him like a land of gold and glory; now it had shrunk to a flat plain of gray despair.

"We'll talk about this here girl," said Joe. "We'll see what right you got to her!"

18

F<small>OR ALL OF</small> a grim hour they talked, therefore, about young Terry Shawn's right to
Kitty Bowen, and by the time Joe had finished his careful analysis, it was plain to
them both that Terry had no right at all.
For, that very day, he had given proof that
he could not command his temper in a
pinch, and so long as he could not depend
upon himself, how could a woman be expected to depend upon him?

Then, gloomily, Shawn stood up and
went to his horse. He saddled and bridled
it with savage gestures of wrath, while Joe
hung on the outer edge of the circle of
that anger. He saw that his speeches had
cut deep, and he wanted to assuage the
pain of the outlaw, but he found few words
to use on this occasion.

"Where you going, Terry?" he asked at
length.

"I dunno."

"Wait a minute. I'll toss a saddle onto
the pinto and come along."

"You got some artist work waiting for
you," said Shawn. "Maybe you can put an-

other curb on the hock of that ostrich—lark, I mean. You stay here; I'll go alone!"

This last was in the tone of a peremptory command, and Joe shrank under it. But, when his friend was out of sight across the hill, he nevertheless saddled the pinto and flew in pursuit.

He had barely rounded the side of the second hill when a rider moved out from the edge of the towering boulders and confronted him. It was Terry Shawn.

"Will you go back and stay at home?" he demanded.

"I'm worried as hell about you," explained Joe. "You got a bad look in your eye, like a gent who's about to chuck his last penny on the table and shoot the dice for it. Now old-timer, no matter what you got in mind, I'll ride with you and stick with you to the finish."

"I've rode alone all of my life," said Terry Shawn. "I've fought alone, robbed alone, played alone, and I'm not going to start working double now. Joe, go back to your home, and don't come after me again. I ask you special!"

He twitched his horse around, as he said this, and jogged it straight on across the hills. After that encounter, Joe dared not pursue, but he sat his saddle for a long time, marking the outlaw in the distance, dipping up and down from sight, again and again.

That course led for Lister, as Joe well knew, and nothing but some most desperate scheme should be carrying famous Terry Shawn toward the town in broad daylight. What scheme it could be, Joe could not guess, but he felt that it must have been brought to mind by the gloomy conclusions of their last talk together. Bitterly did Joe repent now. Kitty Bowen was a very pretty girl, a very kind girl, but, after all, what was her welfare compared with the welfare of such a man as Terence Shawn?

However, he turned back sadly toward his shack, for he dreaded the wrath of Shawn as he dreaded red fire.

He had not been wrong. Straight across the hills rode Terence Shawn, aiming toward the little town of Lister. The afternoon sun was growing into its fullest power, and the vegetation of the earth seemed to be baking and withering under the blast of that oven heat. Yet Shawn paid no attention to the heat. Sometimes he was filled with such wrath against Joe that he wanted to turn about and spur hotly to the shack and pistol his friend in the doorway. But he never could bring himself to such a mad act. He knew that Joe loved him, and all the counsel which the lanky, wise puncher had spoken had been brought forth for his own good; nevertheless, he was ill at ease. Out of the last and most recent treasures of his mind the picture of Kitty as she had been that morning was ever ready to be drawn forth. He saw her so plainly that it almost seemed her ghost was still beside him, cool and damp of cheek, with smiling lips and gentle eyes. He had been through a hundred flirtations; never before had he loved, and the anguish and the joy of it overpowered him. For there was no trace of mental endurance in Terry Shawn. He could ride for days without food and almost without water. He could fight until the last blood left his body. But he could not build a fence against the torments of the mind.

Sometimes he felt, during this ride, that he would soon break through the restraint which wise Joe had placed upon him; and again he felt that he would rather throw away his life than place Kitty Bowen in the slightest danger of future unhappiness even at his own hands. The good and evil angels never tugged so hard at one poor mortal soul as they tugged at the outlaw during that hot ride.

His conclusion was merely that which had flashed across his brain back at Joe's house. He must have diversion. He must have some means of pacifying his outraged nerves and revolting soul, and therefore he would go into Lister—ride into Lister by the open light of day!

The very danger was what intrigued Shawn. He turned to it as another man turns to whiskey in a similar crisis. And is it not strange that man never commits such follies and cries as when his mind has been the least bit unhinged by love of woman?

Now, from the top of the last hill, he looked down into the valley. The town looked half buried in cool greenery, but he knew the terrible and more humid heat which reigned there in the shadows; only in the distance the silver face of the river was alluring, with the broad and clumsy etching of trees against its surface.

A whirlwind began at the upper end of the valley and, covering Lister with a cloud of white dust, left it clean again and circled aimlessly onwards until it disappeared as suddenly as it had risen.

"That's the way with me today," thought the outlaw. "I'll raise a dust when I come in, and I'll go out like nothing at all!"

He chuckled with a savage enjoyment of that grim idea, and then cantered his horse down the slope. He had made up his mind where he would go in the town—he would go to Lowrie's and there he would stretch his legs in the cool and order a drink, and watch the dice roll and the cards fall. He might even play a little himself!

When he came down from the hill, however, he did not turn to the little back alley which led the secret way to Lowrie's; instead, he cantered straight on down the main street of the town. A dust cloud was pitched into the air before him by a brisk following wind; that mist obscured him too well, and therefore, since what he wanted was excitement, he brought his horse back to a walk; the dust settled; he now was visible to all men.

So he waited, his nerves tingling. Many and many a curious, half-anxious glance was cast toward him, from time to time, but he always managed to pass by before a definite alarm was given out. The slowness of his pace allowed him to drift easily into the view of the passers-by, and friction-less, to pass out of their ken again.

Now, such was the manner in which the outlaw was welcomed in the town of Lister—merely by a few casual turns of the head until he came to the bridge across the river, and on the arch of the bridge sat a small boy chattering with a companion.

"Hey, Billy, don't that look like Terry Shawn, though?"

"Don't it look like Jerusalem. My God, would Shawn ride into Lister in broad daylight? He ain't crazy, I guess."

So the heart of young Terry Shawn lightened a little. He began to smile somewhat to himself, and very confidently he turned to the left on the far side of the bridge, and entered the alley where Lowrie's gaming house stood. He gave the reins of his horse to a Negro boy at the door.

"Stand that horse under that tree, kid, and you stay with him every minute. No matter what happens, you be sure to stay there and be ready to hand me the reins if I come out of this joint again."

Fifty cents sealed the bargain.

"I'll wait there till you grow rheumatism," said the little boy. "Good luck to you and your guns, sir."

The outlaw smiled grimly down upon him and kicked open the swinging door which commanded the entrance of the house of entertainment. He found within a tolerably cool atmosphere, an odor of liquor, a lazy bartender, and half a dozen men more asleep than awake in a corner around a table.

Mr. Shawn strode to the bar and struck upon it with the iron-hard flat of his hand, so that the report as of a revolver rang through the room.

"Stand up on your hind legs and come and get it," he commanded. "Stand up and raise your thirst because I'm gunna quench it, boys. Who'll have a drink with Terry Shawn?"

19

THEY ROSE AND they came swiftly in answer to that call—the boozing yegg, the pair of darkly handsome professional gamesters, the jockey retired from the turf because of certain weird practices when he had the mount on a winning horse, the "treasure seeker" from south of the Rio Grande, filled with wonderful stories and no gold, the

146

hired gunman who wandered across the West waiting until his weapons could be used and dividing the rest of his time between liquor and practice in the arts of drawing and shooting swift and straight. These men arose like shadows, and like shadows they came about the bar, ranging before the slender, brown-faced lad with covert smiles of pleasure. They themselves were not unknown; they had done their share of labor in the name of the devil and they would labor again and again when the opportunity arose, but they had not achieved such a position in the eyes of the world as that of Terry Shawn. He had made crime brilliant, beautiful, a winged thing; young boys and old men read or heard of his exploits with lifted hearts, and because of his gallant course the whole profession of the lawbreaker was elevated.

The gunman in particular rejoiced. He could say, "My partner, Terry Shawn—one day when we was drinking together down in Lowrie's in Lister—"

So thinking, he glided silent as a falling leaf behind the outlaw, and the famous man stirred a little, as though touched with a spur point of suspicion; nevertheless, he hardened himself against the danger and watched the glasses filled by a bartender as furtive, as shifty-handed and covert as any of the guests who stood before him.

And young Shawn beat again on the bar before him and shouted, "Who else is here? Who's hanging around the corner, there? Come and liquor, but don't stay and listen, or you'll be damned before you're five minutes older,!"

And not one, but three men came slowly from an inner room and paused in the doorway while they fixed their bright, small eyes on noisy Terry. Then they stepped to the bar. They accepted their drinks with the left hand. Their manner of taking their potions was by waving the glass briskly to one side and the other, and then tossing off the whiskey with a swift movement, so that the drink was tipped down the throat without making it necessary for them to turn back their heads.

How many a man has been shot through the heart while his eyes examine the ceiling and whiskey goes down his gullet?

"You with the black mustache," said Terry Shawn, "step up here and talk to me."

He repeated suddenly, "You with the

black mustaches and the cat eyes, step up here and talk to me, by God!"

The desperate ring in his voice had its effect. For one thing, it placed him in the most terrible danger, for all that evil crew faced toward him, unafraid, but calculating chances, and their lips working like the lips of beasts above fangs. The little bartender leaned against the bar, touching it softly with the tips of his delicate fingers. He, too, was thinking, and if his thoughts came to a sudden determination, Shawn knew that one gesture would bring guns and knives at his throat.

Nevertheless, no signal was given, and the bloodhounds hung in their traces, and the appointed man stepped slowly forward. He stood close to Terry, tall, unafraid, and out of his curious, animal eyes he looked straight into the soul of Terry Shawn.

"I know you, don't I?" said Shawn.

"Maybe you do, Shawn."

"You're Slippery Joe of Boston, ain't you?"

"You have me wrong," said the other, and his pearly white teeth showed as he spoke. Such are the teeth of a cat—translucent white, and pointed.

"I don't think that I got you wrong,"

insisted Shawn. "You're Boston Joe, the fellow that can run up a pack three times and knock three crimps in it. Miss the first one, and you'll hit the second, and Joe can read them wherever you cut. Is that right, Joe?"

The latter raised a dainty hand—his left hand—and just touched his mustaches. But the first touch against their waxed and polished surface made him remove his hand in haste as though in fear of spoiling that triumph of the toilet.

"You're Boston Joe, all right," continued the garrulous outlaw. "You're the fellow that got the tenderfoot from Manhattan and grabbed his wad—that night down in Phoenix. He shot himself the next morning. You remember?"

"I never was in Phoenix in my life," said the other gently.

"It must of been you," declared Terry Shawn. "Down in El Paso, you're the fellow that rolled the tame pair of dice all night in El Paso—all night, on a blanket and bouncing 'em on one wall. That was the night that you took that San Antone kid; he cut his throat the next day. You remember, Blackie?"

"Blackie" shrank a little, as though the

roughly found nickname offended his delicate soul to the very core.

"I never saw you in El Paso," said he.

"You must be mistaken," said the outlaw.

"I'm never mistaken," answered the other in the same delicate and chilled voice.

"Then why have you got this?" asked the outlaw.

Very swift was "Blackie" and went for his gun with a gesture as fast, say, as a play of light from the face of a little hand mirror; but he was not fast enough for the spirit-like speed of thought with which Terry Shawn reached out and caught the other by the wrist.

Under the iron pressure, Blackie's fingers turned numb and dropped on the floor a shining little automatic—small enough to be hidden in a coat pocket, in a sleeve, say—small and infinitely deadly, with a shower of seven bullets to be launched at a single touching of the finger. That weapon fell, and Terry Shawn clipped it out of mid-air just as it was touching the boards. So an eagle stoops and catches the fish which he has made the hawk disgorge.

"I'm mistaken about you?" said Terry Shawn cheerfully. "But then explain what I see, here?"

He turned the slender hand of the other over on the bar and exposed the soft and folded palm and the long, long, slender fingers.

"Otherwise," said Terry, "how did you get a hand like that? There's no honest work in that. It could pick a watch out of a stranger's pocket. Better still, it could pick the right card out of a pack. Am I right?"

"Blackie" returned no answer. Since he had lost his gun, he showed not the slightest perturbation, and his strange eyes never left the face of the outlaw.

"And so," said Shawn, "suppose that you and I and a couple of others sit down to a game of poker where you can use your arts and I can use mine? What do you say, Blackie of Phoenix and El Paso?"

With this, he offered back the automatic, but he offered it muzzle first, only slowly relaxing his grip on the handle. Blackie accepted the weapon in the same gingerly style in which it was offered, and now the faintest of smiles appeared on his lips—one could hardly say whether it was a smile of purest pleasure or a smile of purest malice.

"We might sit in at a little friendly game," said he.

"And who else?" asked Shawn, stepping back and looking over the crowd again.

At that moment, he noticed another form, not a whit less sinister than any of the others—Jose the Mexican, standing in the inner doorway.

"There's another man with a hand for cards," said he. "Jose, will you make one?"

"Señor, a poor man must do as he is bidden," said Jose, but his glittering eyes belied the humility of his speech.

The five were made up, then, of Jose, Blackie, Shawn, and those two silken-handed gentlemen who had appeared with Blackie from the interior of the house. To that interior room they now returned, all five, and as they settled around the round table, the little bartender like a shadow drifted near them.

"What'll you drink, gents?"

"Something that you'll drink before us," said Terry Shawn. "Something honest, to go with an honest game of cards."

He smiled as he said this last, and the bartender smiled in sympathetic understanding; and all were pleasant and at ease around that table except Jose, who sat stiff in his chair and had grown a little pale.

153

The fire of the gold hunger showed in Jose, then; he was a famished man set at a board which was heaped with delicacies just to his taste, and as the cards rattled in the first deal a shudder ran through his body. He rubbed his hands slowly and violently together. He flexed the fingers one by one, and then he picked up his deal as though each card weighed a pound. Terry Shawn looked steadily across at him; the Mexican flashed back a single glance; they understood one another perfectly.

Indeed, there was singular harmony all around that table. Each man knew that the other four were quite capable of handling the pack with cunning crookedness, and each man trusted that his own skill would be greater than that of the others. The betting was very odd. Men laid down three of a kind without risking a penny. Again, two pair saw five hundred dollars on the table, and five hundred dollars won.

There was no conversation. Bets were laid in silence or with the quiet signal of a lifted finger, and there was no sound other than the light click, rattle, and whisper of the cards. What dealing it was—sometimes all four cards in the air at once, spinning low to the table, hovering, descending like birds, very accurately. The three gamblers were three pillars of ice. Terry Shawn was keenly amused, and the Mexican fierce and tense.

So hours began to drop away. Piles of money appeared, shifted this way and that.

Then Blackie pushed back his chair.

"I'll step out and take a breath of air."

"But you won't come back to this game," said Jose gently.

And suddenly the dealer stopped in the midst of his deal. A little waiting silence dropped upon the group.

20

NOW WHEN BLACKIE had waited his moment, he smiled again and nodded. Then he stood up and left the room. His two fellow gamblers stared after him.

"But he can't pull out like that!" said one of them.

"I'm two hundred down to him," said the other.

"Let's get him back!"

They sprang up from the table.

"Friends," said Mr. Shawn, "that ends the game, you know."

"Don't talk like a fool," said one in hasty answer, as he departed; and the two disappeared through an opposite room.

The bartender laid five drinks, noiselessly, on the edge of the table and withdrew. But as he was going, the long arm of Jose darted out and caught him. The Mexican made an eloquent motion of drinking.

"Have a glass," insisted Terry Shawn. "Drink up, bartender. That's what Jose means.

The little bartender fawned upon them with eyes that wrinkled out of sight, but he shook his head and strove to slip away.

"D'you hear me?" cried Shawn. "Drink up, man. You're not a temperance lecturer, I hope? Take a glass, here."

"Thank you," said the bartender, suddenly changing his mind, and he picked up a drink with a little bow.

"It won't do," replied Shawn. "Not that one, but this here very same glass that you set down before me. I'm gunna give you the honor of having my own drink, d'you hear? So down with it, old soft-foot. Down with it, down with it!"

He rose and stood above the bartender with sinister laughter, and now the little man shrank away before him.

"I'll give you one more second before I pour it down your throat," said Shawn.

Like a cornered rat, silently savage, the bartender shook a knife from his sleeve and drove it straight at the breast of Shawn, but his aim was spoiled by a glassful of burning liquor which was cast into his eyes. Then knuckles of steel rapped him on the jaw and he toppled headlong to the floor and lay still.

"Poison, Jose," said Shawn. "What a fine gang they are! Poison to turn the trick if they couldn't handle the cards well enough."

Jose was long since on his feet, a heavy, old-fashioned Colt in his hand.

"It is time to leave!" he said.

"And how, Jose?"

"By the door, señor, of course!"

"Well, try that way."

Jose stepped to the first door; the heavy click of the lock against the bolt answered the pressure of his hand. He tried each of the other two doors in turn, and each was similarly secured.

They had no time for comment; the voice

of a man beyond the last of the doors now came to them like a purr.

"Terry Shawn!"

"There's my good friend Blackie on the far side of that door," said Shawn. "We'd better have a little conversation with him. Hello, Blackie. Do you want to get back inside?"

Blackie laughed sweetly.

"I'm all cut up about you, Shawn," he said.

"Thanks," said Shawn. "That's real friendly."

"A gunman," continued Blackie, "and the crookedest dealer that ever took a poker deck in the palm of his hand—and yet you walk into a trap like this, Shawn! I'm really cut up. I see that even the cleverest fellows have their weak ideas!"

"They have," answered Shawn. "There's no doubt about it. The cleverest man in the world may be killed with poison or a shot in the back. That's the way that you'll go, for instance, Blackie. Poison, or a knife in your throat while you're asleep."

"Damn you!" exploded Blackie, with a sudden fury and malice. "Say what you want, Shawn, we've got you in our pockets, now, and you'll pay to get out."

"Pay what, Blackie?"

"You and the dirty greaser lifted fifteen hundred from the three of us this evening. We want that money passed under the door."

"And then we're free to go?"

"Maybe you are, then."

"What will be our surety, Blackie?"

"My word of honor," said Blackie.

"Your word?" echoed Shawn.

"Yes."

"Your honor?" said Shawn.

"Then stay there and rot!" shouted the gambler. "I'll do no more for you. Let Lank Heney take charge of you—unless you're lynched on your way to jail, you'll spend the rest of your life wearing stripes, and I'm glad of it."

He departed.

The bartender, at the same moment, recovered a little and crawled to his knees.

Shawn, jerking a thumb at him, said quietly, "Look at that worm, Jose. Go through him and see if he has any other weapons.

Jose obeyed, but his procedure with the little man was strange.

He stood him against the wall and sat in a chair behind him, with the point of a great bowie knife resting against the small

159

of the bartender's spine. Then Jose went leisurely over the clothes of his captive and began to produce a most interesting collection. He took out a second knife, the twin brother of the first weapon with which the little fellow had attacked Shawn. Then he took a short-nosed, two-barreled pistol, very small, but throwing a large bullet—one of those guns which kill effectively enough at ten paces and yet make hardly enough noise to break through the sound of conversation and laughter in a room. There was, also, a very small automatic of minute bore; it would make a wound hardly more than the thrust of a needle but passing through body and bone to the life.

"Murder!" said Jose gravely. "This is a murderer, señor. Do you know what we used to do with such men in Mexico?"

"Tell me, Jose."

"We stripped them and threw them into an ocatillo; the thorns killed them in one way and the sun killed them in another. They were spitted and roasted. And this devil would die well, like that!"

"A good idea," said the outlaw, "but we can't spare him now. 'We're inside the can, Jose, and we have to use him as the can opener. Blackie and the rest probably have sent for the sheriff, by this time."

Jose grew a pale yellow.

"Listen to me, Shorty," said Shawn to the bartender. "There's a way out of this room, I've an idea. Suppose that you show me how, and we'll call it square between you and me.

Shorty sat down in a corner and folded his arms and closed his eyes.

"Stubborn," said Shawn briefly, and began to clean his guns, though they were already polished brightly.

Jose strode swiftly and restlessly back and forth through the room.

"'We could smash the lock of one of these doors and rush them," said Jose.

"It works in books but never in fact," answered Shawn. "All they want is a chance to turn loose on us if we try to break away. No, no, Jose, they got all these doors watched."

Jose began to sweat copiously and his fingers worked in and out.

"Do we do nothing, señor?"

"We only wait for Shorty, here. He'll change his mind pretty soon. You understand, Shorty? The minute that the sheriff arrives, I send you to hell before us."

At this, Shorty's eyes opened as far as they were able and stared at the outlaw.

"Otherwise," said Shawn, "you show us the way out and go safe yourself."

Shorty smiled.

"You don't doubt my word, Shorty?" asked the outlaw. "It's better, my son, than gold in the wallet."

At the same moment, there was a sound of many feet in the outer hall, and then the well-known nasal voice of the sheriff. "Where are they? Back here? Loftus, this is a good day's work for you. You'll take half the reward, if I land him. Have you got the doors watched?"

Apparently the answer was satisfactory; there was a noise of scattering footfalls.

Here Shawn produced a Colt and leveled it.

"How do you take it, Shorty?" he asked. "Sitting down, or standing? The sheriff has come, y'understand?"

"It's murder!" said Shorty, leaning forward and gripping the edge of his chair.

"Better than poison," said Shawn. "A good deal better than that, old-timer."

"Nothin' but a knockout drop," declared Shorty, beginning to tremble.

"Sure," said Shawn, "and a cut throat

after the dope started working on me. No malice, Shorty. But I've told you what to expect."

Shorty threw up a hand.

"Will you give me one chance?"

"Of course."

"Then wait a minute."

The bartender stepped to a corner of the room and there dropped to his knees. He fumbled for a moment, and presently lifted up a board three feet long and six inches wide. Another and another came away in his active hand, and, leaning beside him, Shawn looked down into a deep, dark pit.

Here a hand beat on the door.

"You inside!" said the voice of Lank Heney. "We've blocked every way out. 'Will you use sense and surrender, Shawn, or do we have to smoke you out?"

21

KNEELING BESIDE THE gaping mouth in the floor, Shawn canted his head to the side and listened.

"D'you hear, Jose? The old sheriff is drawling away like he was talking about the weather. Mind you, if ever we have trouble with any man, it's apt to be old man Heney. He goes about a manhunt the way most folks would go about a cup of tea."

"In the name of holy San Guadalupe!" exclaimed the Mexican. "They will break through the door in another moment!"

His leader shrugged his shoulders.

"I'll go first," said the bartender. "I'll show you the way—"

The hard hand of the outlaw caught Shorty by the shoulder and spun him half-way across the room—then Shawn dropped a lighted match into the cavity beneath him; it showed a short drop to a platform, and, beneath this, a flight of steps. To the platform, therefore, he dropped, and, scratching a match, he received Jose beside him.

Above, there was a sudden screeching voice, "Lou! Pete! He's got into the underground! He's working out! Lou, get 'im for Gowd's sike!"

"A cockney, after all," murmured Shawn. "Are you ready, Jose?"

"I go mad waiting, señor!"

They sprang down the narrow little rounded tunnel, the Mexican panting at the shoulder of Terry Shawn. In a few leaps they reached the end of the passage and, thrusting up at the ceiling, a section of it jerked open and they issued into the cool and quiet evening of Lister town.

From the house of the gamblers, just behind them, issued a sound of battering and splintering, as though doors were being broken down, and above all was the screeching of Shorty, who seemed to have turned demoniacal with fury. They stood in a patch of shrubbery which shielded them shoulder high, but, looking over or through the brush, they could see people hurrying to come to the saloon and discover the cause of the disturbance, and round about the place were obviously the sheriff's men, naked guns in their hands, and the determination to use them in their faces.

"This way, this way!" said Jose eagerly. "We can get into the back yard of that house and then—"

"Teddy Morgan has joined the manhunt," said the outlaw curiously. "Teddy Morgan wants the blood money, too—there's his pride and joy—there's his bay mare, Jose! Damn the back yard! I've a mind to ride out of Lister on Teddy's bay.

"Señor Shawn, I tell you—"

"Go the back way, if you wish. I'm going down the main street of Lister. If they get me, they're welcome to me; but I got to have a touch of fun, Jose. I'll meet you at your shack, if you can break through. Go ahead—I'll pick my time!"

Jose cast one earnest look at his companion; then he turned without further question and vanished silently through the brush. Shawn, watching that operation, thought to himself, "He that steps like a cat may act like a cat—the greaser has claws!"

Then he turned his attention forward to the saloon.

The crowd about it was growing every moment, for Lister had finished its day's work, and now it thronged to take in the show. There was a magic circle drawn fifty yards from the house, but outside of that line the crowd gathered and packed together, men, women, and children. They swarmed even on the verge of the shrubbery, and as they began to pour about his hiding place, Terry Shawn simply stepped out and mingled with them.

Their eyes were all forward; he slipped among them without drawing so much as a glance, and so he came to the inner edge of the throng just in front of the saloon at the same time that there was an outbreak of loud voices behind the place—and the nasal, ringing cry of the sheriff, "This way, boys! They've come out of ground here!"

So, at the last, they had worked their way down the tunnel and come out in the patch of shrubbery!

Shawn could hear the screaming voice of Shorty, as he yelled hysterically:

"Oh, damn you, didn't I tell you? Didn't I tell you what they was doing? They're gone! They're gone clean! You damn thickheads and saps! You—"

His voice was abruptly stopped to a shrill spluttering, as though a hard fist had landed on the mouth of the informer. In the meantime, there stood Teddy Morgan's fine bay mare, the reins thrown, near the hitching rack. Teddy was an up-country lad who farmed in a small way and ran a few cattle and hired himself out, from time to time. He was a thrifty fellow and he had taken the money of the outlaw more than once in return for a night's lodging; therefore, to have loaned his hand to the state in a manhunt for the sake of blood money was, in the eyes of Shawn, rank treason: it was against the code and the unwritten laws of honor.

Straight out of the throng stepped Shawn, therefore, and, tossing the reins over the neck of the mare once more, he leaped into the saddle.

On foot, he had managed to pass unnoticed, but the instant his feet were in the stirrups, and the keen mare prancing beneath him, some woman's voice screamed in the crowd, "There's Terry Shawn! There! There! Help!"

The crowd fell into confusion. Shake iron filings on a sheet of white paper, and you will see them scatter wildly here, pile into tiny heaps there, run toward the edges in another place. So that heap of humanity ran wild, some driving toward the outlaw, but most of them rushing away. Some pitched to the ground in their haste; others tumbled over the prostrate; but what chiefly concerned Terry was a narrow little lane that opened up through the thick of the press, and through that lane he galloped the mare.

She was a trained cutting horse; he could guide her with the grip of his knees and the sway of his body, which left his hands free to manage two heavy Colts, and as the good bay picked her way daintily through the crowd, swerving lightly here and there, he turned in the saddle and watched for the pursuit.

Behind the house he saw Lank Heney piling into a saddle, and he brought down a gun to cover him. At the last minute he could not fire. For the second time that day he had the man at his mercy, and for the second time he hesitated and turned away. Behind him he heard the wild cry of Morgan as the latter came for his favorite cow pony and found it gone; and Shawn laughed in a savage content as he pitched the mare into the open and let her race away down the street at last.

Bullets began to sing. He looked back and saw three or four men on the verge of the crowd, two kneeling and others standing, who were opening fire on him. He pitched forward in the saddle and jerked the bay sharply around the next corner of the street.

He was safe, and if the mare was fresh, he would laugh at Lank Heney again on this day! Whether fresh or no, she lengthened her stride beautifully and rushed like leaping water down the street, and with his guns Terry Shawn made game on either side. As he rode, he shouted like a wild Indian, and his guns exploded rapidly: an upper windowpane; the sign of Stevens, the blacksmith; a weather vane over the little bakery; and then he shot at the wooden Indian which for so many years had stood defiant in front of Bowen's General Merchandise Store. Looking back at it as he flew along, he saw that the big nose had disappeared, and Terry Shawn laughed joyously.

The last house of the village jerked away behind him; the hoofs of the mare rang hollow on the bridge which arched a tributary creek of the river, and now he had open country, with only a scattering of little houses, before him.

He was well away, and the mare running like quicksilver, when, looking back, he saw the head of the sheriff's procession just beginning to turn out from Lister, rocking from side to side like the front of a speeding locomotive, and with a steam of white dust spouting high above the riders.

He saw the beating arms as they fed leather to their horses, he saw also that they gained not at all. He would have preferred to turn straight to the left and into the mouth of the first little ravine, but he had promised the Mexican to meet him at his house, and therefore he hugged the bank of the river where the ground was high and the footing of soft, deep turf. So he made good time until he saw the shack of Jose before him. Surely the Mexican never could have got there so soon—but there, beyond all expectation, was certainly Jose, riding out on a roan mustang and leading at the end of a long rope the Sky Pilot.

He waved to the oncoming outlaw; at that gesture, the stallion pitched sharply back, jerking the rope through the hand of his master and flinging the end of the lariat high into the air.

But as it came down in snaky wise, and as the chestnut pitched forward, ready to run, Shawn came under like a bolt from the blue and caught the dropping rope in mid-air.

"Oh, well done, my brother!" cried Jose, as they straightened down the trail together, the led horse galloping lightly at the end of the rope. "I should have killed him before I left him behind for the others to take. Well done, Don Terry. We have our wings with us, and, who knows? We may learn how they may be used before the end of our ride!"

"Let the roan run," commanded Shawn tersely. "That's the important thing!"

The roan could run. Freshly stolen by wise Jose as he slipped through behind the houses to make his escape, he had not picked the worst horse in Lister, and now, matching strides with the bay mare, they saw the smoking train of riders behind them checked, and then forced back.

"It only takes a small crowd to kill off the best horse in the world," observed Jose, looking back in turn. "They are in our hands, señor. Which way shall we ride?"

"Straight up the valley."

"That goes into Bowen's place; he is not friend to you!"

"It goes to Bowen's place, and that's where I *want* to go. Keep on."

22

So THEY STREAKED on. They left the open; the trees began to rise about them, and the trail wound in and out along the trunks; the noise of the hoofbeats behind them came to them in pulses—loudly in the open, veiled and muffled as they entered the woods again.

"The roan?" asked Terry Shawn.

The Mexican threw his hands out in a wide gesture.

"The roan says that I am nothing on his

back, señor. I am a feather and he is a bird. He laughs at such a burden. And the mare?"

"She feels as strong as a rock," answered the judicious outlaw, "but," he added, looking down to her dripping flanks, "she is a little soft. Damn men who won't grain their best horses! They're not worth stealing, Jose. However, I think we have that lot beaten!"

A long gap opened before them. They were well across it and entering the woodland on the farther side before Lank Heney appeared, at the head of his procession of vengeance, now, and riding like a jockey, with all his long frame doubled to the work.

Jose marked him specially.

"I shall persuade him to turn back?" he asked, touching the rifle which was holstered beneath his knee.

"Let him be! Let him be!" said the outlaw briefly. "This ain't his day to die. Keep straight on, Jose. Here's the lead rope. Don't turn even if I turn. Keep straight up the valley!"

They had issued from the trees again, and before them, to the left, was the wide front of the Bowen house, with the brightly colored pattern of its garden spread in front. But, most of all, what the keen eye of the outlaw marked was a woman in sunbonnet and apron on her knees, trowel in hand.

He cast one glance behind, as he galloped for the Bowen house.

Jose rode hard and fast up the valley, but, as one man, the entire posse had swept to the left and followed Terry Shawn. He was the prize in their eyes; what blood money was on the head of the Mexican? And still Lank Heney rode in the forefront, jockeying his tough little horse along and giving nothing away. However, there was a broad gap between him and his goal, and that gap might enable Shawn to do what he wished to do.

He saw Kitty Bowen—plainly it was she, now!—turn and run toward the house. But she hesitated and turned back as he shouted. He saw Bowen himself run from the house onto the front porch, with a rifle in his hand. The screen door slammed loudly behind him, and the merchant raised the weapon to his shoulder. He had left his store on this one day, it seemed, and broken the long habit of years; he was there to guard his girl from such another encounter as she had had that same morning!

"Keep off! Keep Off!" Shawn heard the man cry.

He merely set his teeth, and, steadying the mare, he put her at the front fence and jumped it cleanly. High in the mid-flight of that leap, the rifle clanged; it was as though a hand had snatched the hat from the head of Terry Shawn, and the long hair blew backwards as the mare came down inside the yard.

And there was Terry leaning from the saddle above Kitty Bowen. Her father, on the veranda, his rifle clutched hard, twice raised it to his shoulder, and twice he lowered it again.

"Do you hear, Kitty?" said the outlaw. "I've thought the thing over. I'm not fit for you. I've tested myself. And I couldn't stand the test. I've showed that my word's no good. And I'm going to leave you free. There's ten thousand men all worth more to you than I am. God bless you, honey. Forgive me; forget me! I'm gone!"

He leaned lower, kissed the pale face which stared up to him, and started the mare away with a deep thrust of the spurs. He could not swing to the right and out of the yard in that direction, for the sheriff was rushing close behind him, but, instead, he bolted down the side of the house, leaped the rear fence, swerved among the sheds behind the place.

Then, bearing to the right he headed up the valley again and thanked the kind fortune which made the sheriff follow blindly, like a bulldog, in his tracks. The whole front portion of the parade had gone with Lank Heney. And a year of time and trouble would be needed to repair the damage which plunging hoofs had done to Mr. Bowen's garden.

Only the rear of the stream of riders had not had time to get up with the house, and these swung to the side and made straight on after the flying mare and her rider.

Behind him, too, came Lank Heney and the rest of his best-mounted riders. A few had come to grief at the fences; but four or five remained in the race, and these bunched with the dozen or more laggards who so unexpectedly found themselves up in the forefront of the chase.

They were in good pistol shot, now, and as the least speedy horses in the posse began to fall back once more, while the mare straightened up the ravine, the riders pulled their Colts and opened with a shower of bullets. There was no defense except for Shawn to lie on the neck of the mare and trust to his good fortune.

Certainly her strong heart could be trusted! Unfalteringly she strode. Her neck and shoulders had been whipped to a lather by the chafing of the reins, and the sweat ran from her like water, but still she kept in her stride and held her head straight and long before her, as a good horse should. So that the heart of Terry Shawn swelled a little, and an odd moisture stung his eyes.

He was growing old and weak, he felt, or else he could not have been half unnerved by this most ordinary spectacle of a horse giving its lifeblood for the sake of a casual rider, a man never seen before, never to be seen again; it was enough that the life was asked, and there it lay in the palm of the hand to be taken and used by any scoundrel, any ruffian!

He had crossed the wide-open stretch above the Bowen house, now, and the woods were just before him, but, jockey the mare as he would, he was unable to draw her ahead of the pursuit. Only her brave, generous spirit enabled her to keep any semblance of a gallop, and, though it was true that she had beaten off the great majority of the riders who followed, still Lank Heney on his iron-limbed mustang and five other men close behind stuck in the traces of the mare, and now, bitterly the outlaw admitted it, they were gaining. It was not swift or sudden eating up of the distance. It was no more significant, say, than the slow gathering of flesh into the mouth of a bulldog, as he throttles his enemy. And Shawn felt that his last day surely had come. Certainly his last hour, unless a miracle happened! Ay, but there are miracles at hand for good men and for bad.

Out of the dense copse before him, Shawn saw the twinkle of the sun on a long rifle barrel, and then the weapon clanged. His Colt had come into his grip at the first sight of that pointing danger, but the instant the rifle cracked, he knew that it had not been aimed for him; and far behind he heard a loud yell of pain.

He glanced under his arm, and saw one of the posse trying to pull up his mustang with one hand, while the other arm dangled foolishly, helplessly beside him. Still Lank Heney and the rest poured on, and a simultaneous crash of guns answered the single bullet. A twitch of Shawn's shoulder and another at the side of his coat told him that he had been shaved twice by peril. Then the rifle rang before him again, and, once more glancing back, he saw a horse and man go down in a heap. The rider, spun head over heels, came blindly staggering to his feet again, only to pitch on his face and lie still—badly stunned, beyond a doubt, and very lucky not to have broken his neck in such a fall.

Even the resolution of Lank Heney was not fortified enough to ride on in the face of such deadly marksmanship as this. There were four fighting men left, but against them they had that hidden rifleman and outlawed Terry Shawn whose value as a gunman was attested by the price upon his head.

Lank Heney, pouring in a close fire with a revolver, swerved to the side, and his three followers turned to the other direction, heading for cover.

So the staggering mare came in under the shelter of the trees, and Jose, laughing like a child with his delight, joined his companion.

The bay mare dropped at once to a dog-trot, and her rider even pulled her back to a walk, and, leaning down, loosened the cinches. Five minutes' breathing might give the bay new life.

In the meantime, he turned to Jose.

"You, Jose!" he said roughly. "Why did you do that?"

The Mexican grinned broadly.

"In my country, señor, we are very kind to wild children!"

23

CHECKED BY THE deadly rifle fire of the Mexican, nevertheless the sheriff did not hesitate long, but forged ahead through the trees in order to come again on the traces of the fugitives. Well and keenly did he hunt for the sign of the two, but, though he ranged well up the ravine, he did not find what he wanted. There were trails, to be sure, but they looked a day old.

The reason was simply that Jose and his companion remained in the woodland covert, and only when their horses were well breathed did they drift to the side of the ravine and take shelter in a little blind corner of the cañon wall. So when the patient sheriff came back down the ravine and combed the forest, he found nothing whatever and was forced to turn his face toward Lister again.

The two remained that night in hiding, for though Jose was eager to go on toward the higher mountains, Shawn insisted that they wait. Fresh horses, he declared, would be better than a long start, so they rubbed down their mounts, and saw to it that they had excellent grass for grazing.

Before it was utterly dark, Shawn tried his hand once more with Sky Pilot.

On the lead, or grazing in the little pasture which they had found, the chestnut was as quiet as a favorite child; even when the cinches were drawn up, he merely grunted and stamped in a mild ill humor. But when the outlaw leaped into the saddle, Sky Pilot tried to climb the heavens. He was checked, somewhat, by the long rope with which Jose held him, but inside that limited radius he fought like a lion. For ten mortal minutes Shawn stuck to the saddle. Then, battered, broken, dizzy, with blood trickling from nose and mouth and ears, he was hurled from his stirrups and lay in a heap. Had he not fallen in loose unconsciousness, he certainly must have broken his neck. Even as it was, Jose had to work over him until the dark of the night was thick about them, and it was not until then that he wakened and sat up with a feeble groan.

Later they sat side by side and smoked, Shawn with his head fallen back against a tree trunk, a very sick man indeed.

"So it was with me," explained Jose. "I was a rider, señor. I laughed at the wild horses which were brought in from the range. Horses which had run free for eight or ten years—but they could not buck off their skins, and they could not buck off me. The chestnut was different. I used to tie him to a tree and try to ride him. But he bucked in a circle around it, and finally I would go down. I had only one care—to fall on the outside of the circle and roll out of his reach. Otherwise, he would have killed me as I lay on the ground. A hundred times I have tried that! You see this left leg is crooked. It was broken below the knee by the Colt. I made splints with my own hands and tied up the leg. For a month, for six weeks, I crawled about and lived like a wolf. I ate roots. I trapped little birds and ate them raw. But finally I could walk again. You see this scar across my forehead. That is where he flung me on a rock. I have had five ribs broken. Three times a collarbone has snapped. I have lain in pain and misery, on account of him, for a whole year, nursing myself, being my own doctor, crawling out in wind and snow to forage like a beast. Tell me, señor, why I have not killed him long ago?"

Shawn was silent. He was almost too sick for speech; and Jose turned toward the place where the chestnut was grazing contentedly and began to curse his horse with a soft and solemn profusion.

They slept, afterwards, and in the gray morning they prepared to ride again.

They left the cañon and journeyed straight across the hills toward Joe's house, where they could find food—and get the latest news; moreover, that was a direction in which they would not be apt to be hunted. On the way, Jose opened his heart.

"You have told me, my friend, of the old man of the mountain who made the chestnut like a child in school?"

"I have. I saw it, Jose."

"Let us go up to him, then. If he has made the horse obedient once, perhaps he can do so again; and we, Don Terry, will watch and learn what he does."

There was no objection from Shawn. He hardly cared what trail he followed now, so long as it led away from Lister and Kitty Bowen.

So they rode in a wretched silence across the hills. There was no fog this morning. Instead, the sky was coated with pale gray clouds, from which a steady mist of rain fell—a cold rain blowing steadily out of the north and turning their hands numb upon the reins. The two saddle horses plodded on with downward heads, as good range horses will do, submitting to misery; but the chestnut danced and pranced through the storm with a heart as light as a feather.

"Why should he be sad?" said the Mexican, gloomily watching the colt. "Men are the masters of everything, and he is a master of men. Therefore he laughs! He is outside the law of horses, señor, which says that they must work and obey."

Now they saw Joe's shack, half drowned in the rain mists before them, and they raised their horses to a gallop until they had come to the door of the little house. Joe appeared at the same instant, dragging in a log for firewood, his mustang hitched to the timber with a line.

He greeted them with a silent wave of the hand.

"Don't talk to him," said Shawn softly to the Mexican. "He's looking black this morning. Every man who lives alone like this has his ups and downs, and Joe is down this morning!"

So with hardly a word spoken, they took their places at the little table and let Joe serve them with food.

It was eaten in the same silence. Only, when they rose to depart, Shawn pressed a little sheaf of bills into the hand of his host.

"Here's a rainy day," he explained, "and here's something to warm you up a little, Joe."

"I don't want it," answered Joe gruffly, and passed back the money.

"You don't understand, old fellow," said Shawn. "I'm flush. I'm not broke, Joe. Take that and you're welcome to it. There are other places where I can drop in and get a meal, from time to time, but I'm never sure of the people. You're the only one that I can count on."

"You've counted on me for the last time," returned Joe.

Shawn tried to smile, searching for the

jest, but the face of Joe remained utterly grim.

"I'm through with you," Joe explained slowly. "I never minded when you raised all kinds of hell except this last kind, Kid. Now I'm finished."

"What kind?" asked Shawn eagerly. "Lifting money from a set of crooked gamblers, Joe? D'you balk at that?"

Joe turned aside with a sneer.

"You know what I mean," he said shortly.

But Shawn followed him and turned him about.

"I got no idea at all," said he.

"The next time," cried Joe in a burst of anger, "when the boys take after you, I'm going to be riding with them, and I'll have my gun on tap. Is that clear to you?"

"What in the name of God has happened?" asked Shawn.

"Nothing," said Joe. "To you it ain't a thing! To take a fine girl away from her home and drag her down to hell—that ain't worth thinking about, to you!"

"Take a girl from her home—what the devil are you talking about, man?"

Joe pointed a grimy forefinger.

"What'd you do with her?" he asked savagely.

"With who?"

"Where did you take her?"

"Will you tell me who you mean?"

"By God," cried Joe, "it makes me hate the heart of you to have you dodge me like this. Who do I mean but Kitty Bowen? Where is she?"

"At her home—where I last left her. Of course she's there!"

"Is she?" snarled Joe. "And that's why old Bowen is ridin' over the hills, with his hair turned gray? And that's why the boys are promising you a rope this time? And that's why I'm going to help them get you, Shawn? Sure—just because you left her at her home, where you found her! Hell, Terry, you don't think you can bamboozle me like that, do you?"

"Kitty Bowen! Kitty Bowen!" breathed Terry. "D'you mean it, Joe?"

Here Jose put in honestly, "It is not true, señor. I myself have been with Don Terry all this day. She hasn't been with us."

"Greaser," said Joe, more savagely than ever, "d'you think that your lying makes any difference to me? The pair of you are cut out of the same kind of cloth, and it's a kind that I got no use for! D'you understand? I've throwed up the chuck for you this morning. It's the last time. Shawn, I never want to see you again, except in jail!"

And, turning on his heel, he stalked out of the house mounted his horse, and rode off into the mist of rain.

Shawn followed to the doorway and looked after him until he was out of sight. Then he mutely signaled to his companion, and led the way back to their horses.

"But it is wrong!" cried Jose. "You have not told them, my friend! You have not explained that they're wrong! She is not with us!"

There was no answer from Shawn until they had covered the first long mile toward Mount Shannon. Then he said sadly, "What good is talking, Jose? What good is the word of a crook? Only—where in Gods name could she be?"

24

THEY TOOK THE first straight trail toward the distant heights of Mount Shannon, and that way took them at once into the mouth of a cañon. It was ordinarily as quiet and commonplace as any of half a hundred ravines that split and wrinkled the face of the big mountain, but now it was transformed. That misting rain which wrapped the plains and the lower hills apparently had fallen in thick and solid torrents on the crest of the upper mountains, so that now a great stream was bounding and thundering down the valley. Pebbles as big as a clenched fist were whirled along close to the surface, and deeper down, where the water was clear enough to be looked through, heavy boulders staggered and turned before the blast of the current. The strong rock walls trembled with the force of the loaded water, and the echoes which bellowed from side to side continually dislodged stones and let them fall from the upper ridges, so that it seemed heavy, invisible feet must be running up and down on either side of the cañon, spurning these stones from their path.

Jose blinked and shook his head at this uproar, but the confusion and the crashing fitted oddly with the humor of Terence Shawn, for heart and brain were lost in his own troubles. He had entered, it seemed, a sort of Twilight of the Gods, and all his life was changed. To his superstitious mind, it appeared that all was linked with his first contact with the chestnut colt. For out of the meeting with that horse had come a long train of evils. Or was it, indeed, the strange deaf mute who lived in the wilderness on Mount Shannon who had put some sort of mystical curse upon him because he took the chestnut away? There was enough superstition in Shawn to make him cringe at this idea.

So beset was his mind with these ideas that he took no heed of anything around him except the crash of the water down the ravine, and the occasional fall of a distant stone down the cañon walls; it was Jose who struck his shoulder sharply and then turned his horse aside from the trail, leaping it into a thicket.

When Shawn had followed and cast an inquiring eye at his companion, Jose pointed, and through the foliage, far down the trail, Shawn could see two riders hurrying up the valley.

"Headhunters!" said Shawn savagely. "By God, Jose, we'll talk to those fellows. Head-hunters, Jose! Why else would they be riding horses like that?"

For, as the pair drew nearer, it could be seen that they rode magnificent, long-limbed horses, plainly of good breeding, and certainly not the type which usually is used for knocking about through the thickets and the rocks of the mountains.

"D'you know them?" murmured Shawn a moment later.

"I have never seen them, my friend."

"I'll tell you. It's Hack Thomas and Jim Berry. Why, they've worked with me, in the old days. They've been pals of mine. I saw Hack out of Tucson one day when a hundred wild men were trying to take his scalp. I backed him up and covered him until he could get started. There's Berry, too. I've staked him twice; I've worked beside him, too. I say, damn human nature! What difference do the old times make when there's a price on a man's head? No difference at all. Joe, too. He pretends it's because of the girl. Damn his heart, it ain't! He wants his chance to get in on the easy money. The price of a lucky bullet brings in five thousand for him! D'you see, Jose? But I'm going to make that pair wish to God that they'd never rode on my trail! We'll lie low till they get past! Look at 'em! They're reading my trail!"

So said the outlaw, his fury growing fast, for as the two came up the trail, it was plain that they leaned from the saddle, time after time, to read the sign before them. They came closer—two tall, thin-faced, dark men, enough alike to have passed for twin brothers, although Thomas was the older of the two, each riding with a matchless grace, each armed to the teeth with bowie knife, revolvers, and the inevitable long Winchester which usually was carried in the holster under the right leg but which these hunters now kept exposed, balancing the weight across the pommels of their saddles.

They jogged their horses past the thicket when Shawn, having dismounted, stepped from the shrubbery onto the trail behind them, a revolver balanced in either hand. Jose remained in cover, his rifle at his shoulder, prepared for emergencies. But the last stern word from Shawn was, "This is my game. Hands off!"

"Hack!" shouted the outlaw.

Hack Thomas and his companion whirled their horses about with exclamations of astonishment; they found themselves under the cover of Shawn's two steady guns.

"Hey, Terry!" cried Thomas. "We been looking for you!"

"Sure you have," said Shawn. "I could

see that. Maybe you wanted to give me a cup of tea, or something. Or you just rode up here behind me to pass the time of day, maybe? Is that it?"

"He thinks that we been after him," said Hack grimly. "How're you gunna persuade him, Jim?"

Mr. Berry bit his lip.

"Why, Shawn," he said, "you know me, old-timer?"

"I ain't drunk," declared Shawn. "Neither are you. If you were, it'd make it easier for you to take what's coming!"

"And what's coming?" asked Berry, with more curiosity than fear.

"I'll give you both an even break, one after the other," answered Shawn, "but I'm gunna have this out with you here and now! You hear me talk?"

"I hear you talk like a fool," broke in Hack Thomas. "D'you think that we're after the reward?"

"You'd be above it, I guess?" sneered Terry Shawn. "What's five thousand to a pair of high-minded gents like the two of you?"

"What's five thousand compared to fifty thousand?" said Jim Berry, still calm of eye.

"You can't make a fool out of me!" declared Shawn.

"We can't," said Berry. "You've done that before for yourself. What in hell is eating you? If we did drop you, how could we collect? D'you think that they don't know us? D'you think that we're not wanted, kid, near as bad as you?"

"Only," admitted Thomas, "we didn't ever make a play like yours, kid. We got no flower in the buttonhole. We never sneaked girls away from their homes. What's come over you lately? That ain't your old style!"

Shawn, in doubt as he listened, drew back a little, watching them with a hawk-like sharpness, and neither of them stirred hand or muscle under that scrutiny. To have moved so much as a finger meant death, and they seemed to know it perfectly well.

"I want to believe you," said Shawn gloomily. "I want to believe that you boys didn't come up here to get me!"

"Go ahead and believe it, then," grinned Thomas. "We won't hold you back. And just shove those Colts away in your clothes, kid. It makes me feel terrible sick to look at 'em!"

"Jose," said Shawn, "keep a sharp watch."

And suddenly he put away his revolvers.

"The greaser is in the brush, is he?" asked Jim Berry, nodding in the correct direction.

"He is," said Shawn, "and he's covering you. I want to trust you fellows, but I can't, just yet. They've been riding me from wall to wall, boys. They've got me a little nervous, finally!"

"We've heard about it," admitted Thomas. "That was how we guessed where we'd find you."

"This ravine, you mean?"

"Yes, because it's the shortest cut to the tall timber. Terry, we need you bad. We got a little proposition to put up to you! That's why we're here."

"Business?"

"It is."

"What kind?"

"You want us to talk with Jose listening?"

"Aye, fire away."

"Bank stuff, Terry!"

"I've quit teaming," said Shawn. "I do my stuff alone. You ought to know that!"

"Sure you work alone. But this deal is different. Said fifty thousand, kid!"

"As much as that?"

"That's the least it can be. It ought to work to a hundred and fifty. Now, kid, does that sound big enough for you to have a share in it?"

"Oh, damn the money!" answered Shawn gloomily. "But if there's any excitement to be had out of it—I dunno, Hack. It might tempt me a little!"

"Excitement?" murmured Hack Thomas. "Well, all you got to do is to ride into a town with us in broad daylight and help us stick up the bank. How does that sound to you?"

"Where?"

"Kline River."

"You mean the new bank?"

"That's it."

Terry Shawn sighed.

"They're loaded with cash," he said, "if you can only make the cashier toss out what's in the safe."

"We got the cashier fixed, kid."

"He's a percentage boy, is he?"

"Cheap. Twenty per cent is all that he wants. Kid, throw your leg over your horse and come along with us now.

Temptation made Terry Shawn's eyes glitter, but suddenly he answered, "It sounds to me, boys. But I got another job on now. Come up the mountain with me, spend a couple of days there, and then maybe I'll ride down with you!"

25

THEY BECAME, IN this fashion, a party of four, and as such their status was altered. They established a point ahead, with one man riding at it; they established a point behind, for a rear guard, and in the center journeyed two; now let Sheriff Lank Heney and his men beware. For, in the first place, they would hardly he able to surprise a party riding in this circumspect fashion, and in the second place, they had numbers sufficient to hold off the challenge of a large body of armed men. Jose was given the rear guard, the post of honor; Hack Thomas journeyed ahead; and in the center were Jim Berry and Shawn. They could afford to close their eyes, as it were, and center their attention on talk.

There was much useful information to be had from Berry. His first advice to Shawn was to clear out of that section of the country as quickly as possible.

"Why?" asked Shawn. "I've done my

work around here. I've made my friends around here. Why should I clear out?"

"Up to yesterday," said Berry, who was a crisp-spoken fellow, "you had as many friends as any long-rider in the world; but today you ain't got three men outside the profession that would stand up for you."

"Go on," murmured Shawn, frowning.

"It's the girl," said Jim Berry. "People won't stand for that. Rob ten banks, if you please, and shoot up a couple of dozen punchers of all kinds. But you ought to leave the women alone, kid. How the hell come that you didn't know that, anyway?"

Terry Shawn turned a dark crimson and his temples throbbed with rage, but there was something about the cold, steady eye of Jim Berry that discouraged a tirade. Besides, he was baffled and bewildered by these continual charges that he had removed Kitty Bowen from her home. He decided to use calm reason and try to get to the bottom of the matter.

"Kitty Bowen's left her home?" he began.

Berry nodded, with a quick and rather ugly side glance at his companion. It was very plain that, had it not been for the need he and Thomas had for the expert assistance of this gunman and robber, he would have been hardly more kindly to Shawn than the others who ranged on his trail.

"She's gone," said Berry. "Well?"

"Look here, Jim, was I ever a girl-chaser?"

Berry shrugged his shoulders, like a man who makes no admission.

"Matter of fact," said Shawn eagerly, "d'you ever know me to have hardly anything to do with 'em?"

"I heard somethin' down in El Paso," said Berry, "about a couple of Mexicans that had come gunning for you because of some damn little señorita—"

"Oh, that was south of the river," said the guileless Shawn, shrugging all guilt from his shoulders.

"Down in East Texas I heard about a girl that tried to foller Terry Shawn back to—"

"I was away on a vacation," said Shawn anxiously. "I mean, I've never bothered the girls around this neck of the woods, Jim."

"Maybe not," said the other grudgingly.

"Now, I ask you, would I be fool enough to bother a girl like Kitty Bowen, who has a thousand admirers—who is known everywhere?"

Berry grunted.

"Would I chuck myself into danger like that?" said Shawn with increasing vehemence,

"She's gone," said the other with a brutal indifference.

"My God," cried Shawn, "what has that got to do with me? Have I got her with me? Is she in my pocket? Did I hide her in a hole in the ground? Or do you think, Berry," he added, with a sudden touch of horror, "d'you think that I—that I murdered her?"

The latter turned a little in the saddle and stared into the wide eyes of the youth. Then he nodded with an air of relief.

"You didn't do that, kid," he declared. "I can see that you didn't do that. But there's such a thing as meeting a girl and naming a place for her to join you later on.

"You think that?" asked Shawn, with his lower jaw thrusting out formidably.

"Don't jump me," said Jim Berry. "I'm not turning you down. I've come up here to get you in on a big job where I need you. The point is, you got to Lister and you make a dead set at Kitty Bowen. Go out and see her at her house. Ride in under her old man's rifle to have ten words with

200

her. And the next morning she's gone. Well, kid, what are folks going to think, unless they got eyes and no brains in their heads?"

This evidence, the outlaw considered with gloomy silence, for he saw that he could make no retort.

At that point, there was a call from Jose, in the rear, and he came up, flying, and announced that he had spotted a horseman who was following them in the distance.

Either they would have to turn aside and let the rider pass, or they must increase their pace, or else drive him away.

"Try a scare," suggested Jim Berry. "Throw a bullet between the front legs of his hoss. Is there only one rider?"

"There is.

They went back to a point of vantage, all three, and they saw, presently, the rider of whom Jose had spoken. He seemed in the distance a small man, narrow-shouldered like a puncher who had spent his life in the saddle, and with a disproportionately huge gray sombrero of the cone-shaped Mexican fashion.

Shawn, being the most certain shot in the group, was chosen to do the shooting.

He dropped on one knee behind a rock and delivered his bullet exactly where Berry had suggested—at the very feet of the stranger's horse.

The mustang pitched up high in the air; but, instead of bolting for cover or turning tail and retreating at full speed, the stranger took off his hat and waved it wildly about his head.

"Mocking us, by God!" said Berry with heat. "There's a cool devil for you!"

Another bullet in the same place made the mustang pitch again, more violently and took him out of sight behind a great boulder—but to the last the rider's hat was violently waved, as in defiance.

The three fugitives looked gravely at one another, and then proceeded up the trail again. They discussed this event seriously. It was a mere boy. So much Jose, whose eyes were like the eyes of a buzzard, was willing to swear. But a mere boy could be more dangerous than any grown man—as Billy the Kid had demonstrated for all time. A grown man possessed an element of reason which prevented him from taking certain risks, but a boy was a mad creature who held headlong to his course no matter what obstacles arose.

You never could guess what a boy would do next!

Therefore, in view of the fact that the young daredevil had defied them so boldly, they determined that they would put a quick stop to him if he showed near them again.

They had not gone another two miles up the cañon when Jose brought swift word that the same pursuer was dodging them from the rear.

Terry Shawn flushed a little.

"It's only one man, boys," said he. "I'll just drop back and argue with him a minute. You wait for me up here."

Jim Berry chuckled without mirth.

"You'll go back and kill that gent or get yourself shot up?" he said. "Damn it, Shawn, you're only a kid yourself—no real sense. No, sir, we'll stop the kid and we'll do it without blowing his fool head off. Jose, can you put a slug through his horse?"

Jose grinned in appreciation, and the three drew back to the edge of a little covert of lodgepole pine to watch the performance of this ceremony.

Once more they saw the indomitable small rider come twisting into view near the flashing river, the mustang black and glistening with sweat as it climbed up the difficult trail. Jose took careful aim. "Shoot when I whistle," said Berry. "We got to warn the little fool before we shoot!"

So he put his two forefingers in his mouth and emitted a blast that shrieked loudly down the cañon above the road of the cataracts. The pursuer stopped his horse and jerked up his head so that the broad brim of the sombrero flared up around his face. That instant Jose's rifle clanged and the mustang dropped lifeless, with sprawling legs.

The youth was out of the saddle instantly. His hat fell from his head. Long blond, womanish hair streamed down over his shoulders. Even under this rifle fire he did not turn to shelter, but, snatching a rifle from the holster of his fallen horse, he dropped to one knee and poured a rapid stream of bullets straight up among the pines, the very first of his shots cutting a twig beside the head of no less a man than Terry Shawn himself, and sending the whole trio scampering back through the wood to a safer distance.

"You see?" grinned Jim Berry. "Young enough to be crazy. Oh, I know the type! Jump off a thousand-foot cliff for a bet.

Eat fire. Fight a hundred men. I dunno but it wouldn't of been wiser to send a bullet through him, instead of through a horse!"

To this, Shawn answered with some dryness, "That may be your idea of a game, Berry, but I make it a practice never to shoot at a man out of cover, and I guess that's the rule that we'll all foller so long as I'm with this party!"

Jim Berry turned a grimly challenging eye, at this remark, and he was met by a glance as cold as ice. Sudden silence fell upon the three, but Berry said no more, and Jose, as he fell back to the rear, once more, was smiling faintly.

26

AFTER A TIME Hack Thomas came back from the front and Berry went out to the lead. However, Shawn purposely refrained from mentioning the difference which had occurred between him and Berry; let the story come with all the prejudiced authority of Jim Berry himself. He did, of course, tell the story of the long-haired boy who followed them and had been unhorsed.

Thomas grinned and then grew sober. "Well," he said, "you'll hear from that kid again, and take it from me you'll hear hard! He ain't going to be shuffled off the trail by the loss of one horse. Kid, I tell you that this trip into the hills is a fool's trick. Let's turn right around the way that I want, and slant straight for the town where we have our job staked out!"

For an answer, young Shawn turned in the saddle and glanced back. The Mexican was just coming into view, Sky Pilot beside him.

"You see that horse?" he said.

"Yes."

"What would you give for it?"

Mr. Thomas turned and looked at the flashing beauty, though, of course, the distance was too great for the reading of points; however, even far off as he was, the greatness of Sky Pilot burst upon the heart even if it did not burst upon the eye.

"I'd give two thousand cold, and I got the cash with me," he announced.

"Now," said the other, "when we get to the end of our march I may have a chance to own that hoss. So don't talk nothing to me about anybody else or anything else!"

Hack Thomas took this answer as final and discreetly turned the talk into other channels.

"Where are we going?"

"To the end of the trail," answered Shawn curtly, and fell deeply into his own profound thoughts.

They had no further sight or sound of the precocious young fighting boy who had been driving up behind them. That same evening they came to the foot of the rugged passes which led up the final brow of Mount Shannon, and pushed up a gorge dripping with water that trickled from the sides, welled from every crack, and seemed to creep up from the very rock underfoot.

They came out, finally, upon the little valley which the outlaw remembered so well. The time was just after sunset. They could look down from the eminence and see the lower mountains lost in the night, and all the broad dark plain stretching away to the south, merely tinged with purple. But up here, reflected from the near sky all around, there was a strong and rosy twilight. From the horizon—north, east, south, and west—the radiance sprang upwards, faded in the central sky, and covered the whole face of Mount Shannon with a rosy glory.

So the four, drawing together in a compact group, came up the little valley and they saw before them the homestead which the hermit had made here on the edge of life. The hour was late, but he was employing the light in a strange fashion. He had put together a wooden plow, tying the tough timbers together with sun-dried and toughened withes, and by dint of pressing down with all his weight on the handle, he managed to sink this sort of Egyptian plow point into the rain-softened earth. Before him walked a saddled horse, and from the point of the saddle ran back a lariat which was hitched to the plow beam; patiently the horse worked ahead, and, scratching some sort of a feeble furrow behind it, answered the twitching of the reins, and turned again at the end of the plowland, and came back toward the other side of the little field.

Young Shawn stopped his companion on the edge of the woods.

"Look, look!" he exclaimed. "D'you see the old boy there? D'you see that horse? Tame, ain't it? A sort of a lamb? Now I'll tell you—I never got a day's ride out of that devil without a bellyful of bucking to warm up on. Bucking in the morning was bacon and eggs to him, and bucking at night was like coffee to a tired man. I say it was—because now you look at him, tame as a baby and beggin' for more work! Look at his ears—pitched straight forward like he was eatin' apples. Oh, damn such a man, I say! If he ain't a witch, I'm a sucker!"

This speech was not greeted with a smile. Jose even took off his hat in a sort of odd reverence.

"Señors," he suggested, "that is a holy man—a saint!"

"Saint, hell!" said Hack Thomas. "It's too far north of the Rio Grande for saints to be bred. You can write down that. It's just some wise old shake—why, kid, this is old Shannon, ain't it?"

"It is."

"I've heard about him. Let's go have a look at him!"

They went up the valley from the wood, accordingly, and when he saw them coming, Shannon paused in his work and leaned upon his plow. Then, taking note of the lateness of the twilight, he abandoned the plowing and began to unknot the draw rope. The four greeted him in silence, because they knew he could not hear them, but they waved most cheerfully, while Shawn explained:

"That was a soft brute. Soft and foolish, but now you look at him. Shannon has him hard and wise. Look at his eye! As understanding as a man's! That's Shannon's work."

"Shut up!" said Hack Thomas. "Shut up and look!"

Shannon, in the midst of his work, had paused with the loosened lariat in his hand to wave a courteous greeting to his guests, and at the same moment he was turned to stone, as it appeared, by the sight of the young chestnut horse. They saw him stiffen; then he dropped the rope and went slowly forward.

"Keep back!" yelled Jose in excited Mexican. "Keep back—that horse is a man-eater, señor! Keep back beyond the length of his line!"

The deaf mute did not falter, and Shawn called sharply, "Be still, Jose. Are you going to teach the finest hoss wrangler that ever walked how to handle a hoss in his own home yard?"

Jose, anxious but silenced, fidgeted in the saddle, and even drew out a revolver, so that he would be able to stop the murderous charge of the stallion, if it were necessary to resort to brutal means in the end.

Without the slightest hesitation, Shannon went straight up to Sky Pilot, who flattened his ears and expanded his nostrils when he saw a human coming so straight at him, and then made a little rear and plunge, as though about to hurl himself at the other. Yet he did not advance but suddenly halted, with his legs widely braced and his head stretched out and his nostrils expanding and snorting.

On went Shannon and laid a hand on the starred brow of the beautiful animal. Sky Pilot at the same instant cast forward his ears, and a whinny of joy rose from the very deeps of his heart. He sniffed at the feet of Shannon. He sniffed at his ground-stained knees, at his hands, at his breast, and at his face, and at last nipped slyly at the hair of Shannon's head.

The hermit smiled. He turned his back to Sky Pilot, and to Shawn he made a singularly graceful gesture.

"He's thanking me," said Shawn, "for bringing back his horse. Now, how in hell can I explain? Jose, let go the rope and see what happens!"

"Let go a thunderbolt! Señor, we never will see the colt again!"

"We will, though. Let go and see!"

It was done, and Sky Pilot, after a lofty spring and a plunge or two, began to gallop swiftly around Shannon, shaking his head and pretending a vast fury, but finally bringing up behind the man of the mountain and trotting like a dog at his heels!

27

At Shannon's open fire, they cooked their supper, Shannon coming and going with perfect patience and never showing the slightest irritation when he saw his larder so heavily drawn upon to meet the needs of the strangers. It was a very dark night; there were enough high-flying clouds to shut out the stars, and now and again some downward blast of that wind which rushed through the central heavens came rushing and roaring through the forest in the valley like warnings of danger to come.

They finished their meal and sat about; the fire was built larger, whole logs and small trees being cast upon the blaze out of Shannon's stock of well-dried and seasoned timber, but still he attempted no protest.

"We'll have to pay high for this, suggested Thomas.

"He won't take money," declared Shawn. "I know him; he'd throw your money back at you. He's a queer one, this Shannon is! He won't take money. He trades in skins for everything that he wants! Never uses coin at all."

Thomas fell into thought.

"We could send him up some stuff, like guns and such. Ammunition. He'd need that up here!"

"You try it," said Shawn. "He'll take nothing. I know him, I tell you."

"But," exclaimed Thomas, "then we're just calmly sitting in the limelight here, and soakin' up things that he's worked hard for and that we can't repay?"

"It looks like it," said Shawn. "Except that I've been figuring on the thing, and I'll find a way sometime."

"What way? What way is there that ain't got money in it?" asked Thomas with vigor. "Tell me, Shawn?"

"Money ain't the only thing in the world, I suppose" suggested Shawn with warmth.

Thomas grew logical, which was an irritating habit with him.

"Look here. What have you ever had in your life that you didn't steal?"

Shawn was silent, growing hot with anger.

"I ain't insulting you," the other assured him. "I just mean to tell you that all a man can steal is money or things that you exchange for money. And so, that's all that you got to make a payment down to Shannon. Well, money is nothing to him. So that leaves him outside of us. We can't have anything to do with him. We can't be square with him. If we take anything, we never can pay it back!"

He had warmed to his work, and now he finished with such emphasis that Berry stared upon him, mouth agape. He turned toward young Shawn, forgetting his recent enmity and merely curious to hear what the answer could be.

Shawn had no answer. He reached deeply into his mind and almost felt that he had words to reply with, but in every instance his heart failed him a little.

He said at last, "I dunno, Thomas. I can't sling words the way that you can. Only, I feel that there's something that could be said by a clever talker." He stared gloomily at Thomas, as he repeated, "You can give a fellow a helping hand, Thomas. I'd call that something that ain't money!"

"Sure," agreed Thomas instantly. "You're gunna take this old goat's hoss that he cottons to so close, and afterwards you're gunna wait till he's in trouble so's you can pay him back. Likely that he'll be in trouble up here, ain't it? He's got so many neighbors that'll bother him, eh?"

Shawn's answer was to fall into a passion, so that he leaped violently to his feet and started to burst into a tirade. He swallowed his fury, however; but the effort cost him so much that he turned and hurried away into the darkness.

It left the Mexican, Thomas, and Jim Berry alone by the fire. This had died down a little, but still it stained the hands and the faces of the men with streaks of blood red. They remained subdued and quiet for a moment after the departure of their more famous companion.

Then Jose took up a handful of pine needles and tossed them into the coals. There was a brief crackling and then an arm of fire that wagged high in the air.

"So," said Jose. "My friend, he is that!"

215

He assisted his meaning by throwing up both hands in an aspiring gesture. Then he relapsed into a chuckle.

"Nice feller," said Jim Berry with sarcasm. "Nice even temper. A doggone lamb, he is. Him—he'd melt in yer mouth. I say," he added with greater warmth, "that he's been spoiled. He's been runnin' with people that he could walk over and sink his spurs in, but the time's come when—"

He was distracted by having the heel of Thomas descend with force upon his toes, and, as he turned a furious face on his companion, he was directed toward Jose with a nod. Then it could be seen that Jose was looking gloomily downwards, his brow contracted into a solid shadow.

"The kid is all right," said Thomas with assurance.

"Aw, maybe he is," agreed Berry, massaging his injured foot. "Only, he gets on my nerves a little. It ain't anything I have against him. Only—look how close he was to a fight, just then!"

"That is true," murmured Jose, reassured by this change of tone in the conversation. "But look, friends—it needs a hot fire before iron can be melted. What good is a little yellow flame?"

They broke up their fireside group to clean the kitchen utensils and knives which they had used in their cookery, and when they had finished that necessary duty to their host, they found Shannon waiting for them on the edge of the dim circle of firelight. Behind him was a splendid and shimmering form of black and crimson—Sky Pilot, still at the heels of the hermit.

So Shannon beckoned to them, and, leading the way to his shack, he kindled a lantern there and pointed out four beds which he had made down with pine boughs and hay, with warm skins to serve for blankets. The three thanked him with gestures and turned in, as tired men will. But when Shannon had gone, they conversed softly, as though for fear of being overheard.

Was it fear of them that had made their host treat them with such hospitality? Or was it a sense of hospitable duty which had controlled him? In the meantime, where was Shawn? Gone to walk off his evil temper and try to devise a way of getting the chestnut colt?

This made Berry put the sharp question, "But how will Shawn settle with you, Jose, if he wants the horse? Sky Pilot belongs to you, I suppose?"

Jose laughed softly.

"That is nothing to worry about," he said. "Who is there that can handle the devil—except a saint, my friends?"

On that, they fell asleep, and were not disturbed when Shawn, in turn, entered softly, found his bunk prepared, and turned in.

He slept a short and broken sleep, however, and when the earliest mountain dawn had come, he was up and about once more. Early as he had risen, however, he was later than the trapper. He saw Shannon already in the meadow with a saddle and bridle over his arm and shoulder, and Sky Pilot cantering eagerly toward him.

With bated breath, Shawn crouched behind the pile of newly cut wood which stood beside the shack and watched what was to follow. It was all very well for Sky Pilot to welcome the man on foot; but what would it be when there was a saddle on his back and feet filling the stirrups? A little shudder went through Shawn, and many recently bruised places ached violently in sympathy.

In fact, when the chestnut spied the saddle, he paused with a snort and swept a rapid circle around Shannon. Then, coming up from the rear, he sniffed at the saddle and flattened his ears. Shawn watched with wonder the unhesitant manner in which the lone dweller went about the work of saddling.

There was one major miracle, to begin with, and that was that Sky Pilot stood unroped for the burden to be strapped upon his back. Once he sidestepped and shook himself like a wet dog. But after that he was calm enough while saddle and bridle were fitted on and made secure.

Now for the mounting!

To the amazement of Shawn, the hermit approached the fire-eating colt from the wrong side, and still Sky Pilot endured it. He stood while a clumsy foot was raised and thrust into the stirrup, only twisting his head around and biting softly at the man's arm.

A heave and a sway, and there was Shannon in the saddle at last!

The chestnut crouched suddenly low, ears flattened so that his head had a most snaky appearance, and every muscle of his splendid body standing out as though carved in stone, so great was his tenseness of fear.

Now for the bolt forward or the lunge into the air!

Shannon clucked; the chestnut crouched lower, and now he was urged forward by a heavy thump of a heel against his ribs, Shawn caught his breath; for who will urge on a lightning bolt?

Yet there was no explosion, and, instead, the colt straightened, shook his head as though to resolve his doubts, and then obediently and softly trotted off with his master, who was such an inexpert horseman that, even at that silken gait, he bounced violently in the saddle.

The dark of the morning woods received them, and Shawn stood up with a still greater darkness upon his face; this was such a miracle as even seeing could hardly make him believe!

28

THE SITUATION IN the valley on the seamed breast of Mount Shannon grew rapidly tense. Berry and Thomas pressed for a departure; they had assented to this trip up into the wilderness in order to please a foolish whim of young Shawn, because they wanted his promised assistance in the matter of the bank robbery, but now that they had arrived in the valley and the business of Shawn appeared hopeless and ridiculous, they urged instant departure.

As Thomas put it briefly and vigorously, "You ought to get out of this section of the country where the law is looking for you. We offer to take you through the dangerous ground and get you away to a safe region and fill your pockets with coin besides. You prefer to stay here and look at a wild horse. Why?"

All Shawn could answer was, "The longer I look at that horse, the more I want it! If the old man can use the horse, then maybe I can learn how to."

"The old man has that pony hypnotized," declared big Thomas. "He's got something about him. All the hosses like him."

This was obvious truth; and the patent challenge was: Unless you, also, have a touch of that natural magic, how can you hope to exercise any power over a bad one like the Sky Pilot?

To clinch everything: "Besides," said Thomas, "even if you could handle the chestnut, he ain't yours; he belongs to Jose!"

Shawn could be reduced to a point where he could argue no longer; but he could not be made to leave the valley. So Jim Berry took his companion aside and declared roundly in favor of chucking the more famous outlaw and going after their work without him. He pointed out that all of their plans were perfect. If they needed a third man, they could pick him up somewhere—any hireling gun fighter!

Thomas listened. He was the sort of man who hears everything to the end, and then makes his answer.

"Three is all that we want," he replied. "Four makes a crowd of it. Four men attract too much attention. But three is rock bottom. One man for each end of the big bank room. Number three is the steely devil who shoves his gun under the cashier's nose and paralyzes him and takes the cash away. Neither of us, kid, is good enough to play the part of number three. Shawn is. And that's why we'll wait here for Shawn."

Against this argument Jim Berry fought, but he fought unsuccessfully. for in his heart of hearts he recognized the truth of what Thomas had said.

In the meantime, Jose was dreaming his hours away in the sun over cigarettes, or fishing in the stream with great success.

And Shawn poured in all his hours on the study of Shannon and the stallion. He followed on foot when Shannon rode out along his trap line. He raced and scrambled and tore through trees, up rocky slopes, down sheer pitches, in order to keep his eye on the old fellow and try to penetrate his secret. But always it was impenetrable. Some times he felt that he had come within hailing distance of something in the touch of Shannon's hand, in his manner of sitting on the wild horse—but, in the end, he realized that these thoughts were the worst sort of folly: Plainly, Shannon rarely wasted caresses on the chestnut, and, as for his sitting the saddle, the miracle was simply that he was permitted to so much as mount. No, it was a control of spirit over spirit, rather than of flesh over flesh, and the more he grew irritated and perplexed, the keener became Shawn's interest. What time the stallion was away from Shannon, Shawn improved by striving with all his might to cultivate a friendship, offering choice bunches of seed grass or succulent dainties that appealed to the tooth of Sky Pilot. Yet he never could draw near without having Sky Pilot shrink shuddering away from him. He never came really close without having the stallion toss his head with an upper lip thrust out stiffly and a foolish look in his eyes—the folly of blank terror and dislike.

"What have I done to you, old fool?" Shawn was apt to say through his teeth. And he confided to Jim Berry and Thomas, "That hoss is two-thirds fool. What've I ever done to 'im? But he's scared to death!"

"How many times you tried to ride him?" asked Thomas.

"Oh, half a dozen."

"You weren't wearing spurs?"

"Well, maybe."

"You didn't have a quirt?"

"Sure, I did."

"Well, you ask why he's scared of you!"

Certainly those wild interviews with Sky Pilot had not been of the sort to fill his soul with trust and peace; but on the second evening, Shannon saw fit to interest himself in the hopeless attachment of Shawn to the chestnut.

The outlaw had followed the stallion down the meadows to a spot where the stream entered a pleasant grove and there widened and spread to a still-faced pool, all covered with shadow, and with a long end of a branch thrusting up out of the water like a black skeleton arm. The grass grew long and rank around the edges of this pool, and as every good horse and eager feeder loves changes of diet, so Sky Pilot had come here to vary his food. Shawn, carefully following with a handful of grain and a bit of sugar, strove to slip up to the red beauty.

The maneuvers of Sky Pilot were those of a naturally wicked and cool-headed horse. For he would allow the man to come almost up to him, before he whipped his tail into the face of his stalker and moved on; or he would stand patient and let poor Shawn reach his shoulder, before he swerved just a little, and kept on swerving which mocked and baffled Shawn as completely as a wide gallop across the fields could have done.

He paused, at last, gritting his teeth to keep back the curses, and, half lost in the pattern of the shadows, he was suddenly aware that eyes were watching him. He started erect, ready for trouble, and then he made out that it was old Shannon smiling faintly through the beard that now grew long and gray and descended far down his breast, matched by the almost equally long hair that fell toward his shoulders.

He nodded, when he saw that he was

observed, and came forward at once. Sky Pilot, as though to show his preference unmistakably, flirted his heels toward Shawn, and cantered eagerly to meet his master. Shannon waved the colt aside as though it were a human being, and, going on to Shawn, he took the lean hand of the outlaw in his and led him to the chestnut. It was exactly, thought Terry Shawn, like being presented as a child, but at the touch of that hand awe overcame him and he went gravely forward.

Sky Pilot, as one who would have none of this, whirled off, a crimson streak, but he came back in a wide circle, looped swiftly around them, and halted suddenly before them again, snorting and stamping.

As clearly as with words, he said to Shannon, "That man is dangerous. I know all about him, and he's full of harm!"

Yet the raised hand of Shannon subdued the stallion and, though he trembled violently, he allowed the two to come up, allowed the hand of the master to carry the hand of the outlaw to his muzzle, his forehead—allowed the hand of Shawn alone to pass down his silky neck, though at this Sky Pilot shook his head and whinnied softly to Shannon for help. For half an hour in that darkening place the introduction continued, and then they walked out from the trees side by side—Shawn leading the stallion by the mane.

He could feel that he was under thin sufferance; it was the presence of old Shannon which made the thing possible, and yet that hardly diminished Shawn's delight in this partial victory. Through that tangle of mane he felt the tremor run down to his hand, and it was very like holding a smoking thunderbolt, ready to be launched. Nevertheless, by the delicate thread of Shannon's will, the stallion was held. Some day, perhaps, with his own unaided hand he could do as much!

The spell was snapped by the sudden exclamation of Jose, who came out of the woods with half a dozen fish dangling from his hand and cried out at this sight. Sky Pilot veered away with a neigh, and Shannon went on to catch him for the night and put him away in the shed; while Jose came up to Terry Shawn with blazing, dark eyes.

"What is the trick, amigo?" he asked. "How did you manage to do that?"

"There's no trick," said Shawn, gazing earnestly after Sky Pilot. "It's all in Shannon's head. God knows how he does it, but he seems to have a rope on the colt all the time!"

"Pah!" snapped Jose, growing angry. "I saw you lead him with your own hand. Is that no trick?"

"I'll tell you what," said Shawn, rolling a cigarette, but keeping his glance full on the face of the Mexican, "I'm feeling near enough to winning to want to buy your claim in that horse. What d'you say, Jose?"

"What price?" asked the other sullenly and curiously.

"I can give you a thousand, spot cash. I'll pay you that much, Jose."

"Why should I sell?" asked Jose. "I take him down to a town and charge five dollars a ride. I make two or three hundred dollars a month that way. Why should I sell him, señor?"

"Because it's a dangerous game. You have ten men pitched on their heads. One day somebody breaks his neck. And that man's brother or father or son comes gunning for you."

"I wear a gun also," said Jose scornfully.

"Ay, and you can use it," admitted the other. "You're a straight shooter both ways from the start. But still you know what I

228

mean. It's dangerous. Now, Jose, I'm offering you a fat little stake for that pony! What d'you say?"

Jose's mind was on another matter.

"How much did you pay Señor Shannon to learn the trick? I, Jose, have no money to pay to him."

He said it bitterly, a glimmer of anger in his eyes.

"I didn't pay a penny," said Shawn with perfect truthfulness.

The Mexican snapped his fingers with impatience.

"I am a child," he suggested. "I must believe everything you tell me"

"Believe a thousand dollars," said the outlaw. "How will that sound to you, old son?"

"Damn a thousand dollars."

The patience of Terry Shawn parted with an almost audible snap.

"Look here, Jose, what's your real claim to Sky Pilot? You've told me the yarn with your own mouth. What right have you got to him?"

"I have paid," said Jose slowly, "nearly three years of hell. Who else has paid so much for him?"

"What would a judge say to that?" asked

Shawn. "What new kind of a bill of sale is that, Jose?"

"Dios, Dios!" screamed Jose, growing wild. "You will take him?"

"Steady," urged Terry Shawn. "I'll never take him against your will. I'm just asking you to be reasonable. There's a horse that'll bring you in ten dollars' worth of trouble for every penny of cash that you get out of him. I offer you a thousand bucks. Look here, man—right in my hand!"

He extended the bills, but Jose, with a furious oath, struck the money from that extended hand and turned on his heel.

The bills fluttered slowly down to the ground and Shawn remained transfixed, staring at his hand, at the falling money, and at the departing form of the Mexican. Never before had he endured so much from any man, and by that blow he felt that all the ties which existed between them were wiped away and made as nothing.

29

LET A WOLF smell bear near his home and he will sleep lightly; so it was with Terry Shawn that night in the shack, dozing for a moment and then opening his eyes suddenly and lying with all senses alert, listening to the breathing of the other four that filled the little room. When he heard a little rustling, late in the night, he raised his head silently, and he waited.

A shadow was moving through the dark, something to be guessed at, rather than seen. Something to be felt, rather than heard. He could have sworn that a form leaned above him through the darkness, and, with a ready revolver, Terry Shawn waited. After an instant, the sense of imminent danger became so great that he was about to sweep a hand before him and fire if that hand struck any obstacle, but at that moment he saw a silhouette step into the doorway, and out again into the starlit night.

He followed at once, picking his way in soft silence, with a fastidious care.

Outside the door, he flattened himself against the wall of the house while he enjoyed a few deep breaths of the cold, pure outer air. Winelike, it made his blood leap, blew the dimness of weariness out of his brain, and made him perfectly alert and collected.

A thin night mist covered the woods so

that it was hard to tell which was forest and which was fog, save that close by the black trunks seemed stepping toward the shack. Overhead, through wide pockets in the mist, he saw the stars hanging as if from wires out of the thick black velvet of the sky. There was not a ghost of wind; there was not a murmur of sound, except an occasional stamp and rumble from the horse shed. Very late for the horses still to be standing!

So thinking, he looked to his revolver again, spun the cylinder, weighed the weapon with affectionate familiarity, and then stole around the edge of the shack and the horse shed.

He was barely in time. Jose had not many moments the start, but Jose worked fast, indeed. There he sat on a saddled horse— Shawn's own mount he had selected for this occasion—and behind him he was drawing Sky Pilot out of the shed door at the end of a long lariat. Unwillingly the stallion came out into the cold of the night, with flattened ears and expanded nostrils.

"Hello, Jose!" said the outlaw.

"Dios!" groaned Jose, and, dropping the lead rope, he fired from the hip.

Good reason had Terry Shawn for commending the accuracy of the Mexican with firearms, but if he had seen no proof of that skill, he could have a testimony in person, hereafter. At the first stir of Jose's hand, he had dropped toward the ground, but even so the skill of Jose, shooting by starlight, sent a bullet that clipped open the shoulder of Shawn's coat, cut through the tail of the coat, and blew away half the heel of his boot. Also, before he struck the ground in falling, Shawn sent in his own fire.

That bullet ended the battle, for it apparently struck Jose in the right arm or shoulder. Out of his hand, the gun dropped to the ground, and leaning well over the saddlebow, flattening himself like an Indian, Jose drove away through the night. The mist opened its arms to receive him.

"Jose! Jose! Fool of a Mexican!" shouted Terry Shawn. "Come back! I'll do you no harm! Come back, Jose! You're hurt! Come back!"

But Jose was gone. The mist seemed to whirl in a thin wave over the spot where he had disappeared, and the dull, hollow echo of his own voice came back to Shawn in empty answer. Other noises, of course, joined in. The three sleepers rushed from the house, active Jim Berry in the lead, a Colt in either hand.

He found Terry Shawn closing the door of the horse shed and in a most uncommunicative humor.

"What's happened, Terry?"

"Jose wanted a little exercise by night," said Shawn slowly. "I just gave him a little send-off!"

Berry wasted no further time in questions. He gave one glance at Terry's downcast head and then stepped past him and opened the shed. By matchlight he made his examination and came out to report to the other two; Terry Shawn had gone quietly back to his blankets.

"Sky Pilot is loose with a lariat around his neck, and Terry's own nag is gone. Jose must of tried to get away with both of them. Think of the fool! To steal Shawn's own horse!"

He whistled softly.

"There you are," announced the philosophical Thomas. "That was a good Mexican. Enough grit to supply a couple of bears and a painter; hard as nails; straight as they come; but too doggone changeable. Lovin' the kid one day; tryin' to murder him the same night!"

Old Shannon went into the shed to examine things for himself.

"Nothing better could have happened," declared Jim Berry. "The kid has been hanging on here, wasting his time. Now he'll have to move, because it's a cinch that the Mexican will never stop till he's brought trouble back to us."

"He'll *have* to move," agreed Thomas. "Listen to that!"

Out from the stable came a soft, deep-throated whinny, such a word as a horse speaks to a dear friend.

"Poor devil!" whispered Thomas, "and he can't speak a word back to that colt. It'd break your heart, Jim, wouldn't it?

So, now that a double death scene had been averted, like true Westerners, all went calmly back to sleep, and not five minutes after his gun had sent a bullet into poor Jose, Terence Shawn had closed his eyes in profound slumber. Thomas and Berry paused in the doorway to listen to the soft snoring of the youth.

"That's nerve," said Thomas in quiet reverence. "Most likely he had a bullet fanning his ear; most likely he shot the liver out of that Mexican; and now he's sound asleep again. He's a lamb, Jim, ain't he?"

Jim agreed with a gloomy murmur; nothing could make him admit much good in the character of the "kid."

Neither did Shawn speak a word about the fight, in the morning. The treble damage that his clothes and boot had suffered spoke for themselves, but since nothing was volunteered, nothing was asked by his two companions; as for old Shannon, he seemed above an interest in such things, and made an early departure to ride the round of his traps.

That day the upper crests of Mount Shannon were lost in a gray shawl, and far to the north the fringes of that garment flecked and flickered across the sky. Snow undoubtedly was falling, yonder on the heights; and though wind was from the south, it seemed a cold wind. By noon the creek had lost half of its volume, and Thomas pointed out the cause.

Up there on the heights the snow was pounding down in thick layers; the melting which supplied that stream had stopped. Before the next morning, no doubt, a heavy freeze would lock the whole upper reaches of Mount Shannon in the first embrace of winter. And, indeed, at any time a heavy fall of snow might wrap the great mountain in white, fall down its sides, and make the rocky trails terribly perilous, and fill the bottoms of the ravines with great wind drifts of crusted white, impassable for man or horse.

"It's time to start, kid!"

"It won't snow! It's just a touch of cold," said Shawn, biting his lip.

"Then look there!"

As if by special intent, the wind, shifting a little, opening the gray mantle that hid the shoulders of Mount Shannon, exposed now a dazzling patch of white which instantly was veiled across again.

"Now what do you say to that?" exclaimed excitable Jim Berry. "Good God, man, are you going to wait to be snowed in, here?"

For answer, Shawn walked sullenly away, his head hanging a little as in thought.

"It's too damn much," said Thomas, touched at last. "Let him go; we'll try for a third man somewhere else; the kid's gone crazy!"

30

THE COLD INCREASED every moment. It thickened the mist which kept pouring up from the south through the trees, it set the horses trembling in the meadow and herded them into the lee of the trees, it filled the solidly built shack with a damp, disheartening chill.

When Shannon came back, in the midafternoon, his first greeting was an eloquent gesture toward the mountaintop, and then, by signs, he indicated that the snow which was falling there might soon be heaped thick along the floor of the valley. Thomas and Berry, ready to be impressed, tried the last appeal to young Shawn, but Terry refused to answer.

"We've waited a long time," said Thomas, biting his lip with angry impatience. "Tomorrow morning we start, old son! Think it over tonight, will you?"

Terry Shawn nodded, but plainly his heart was still too strongly bent upon the stallion. The horse was no sooner back from the round of the traps that day than he went out to work over him.

Slow work, slow work for Terry Shawn!

He could not stalk Sky Pilot; but when he found the section of grass on which he chose to graze—for the cold weather seemed to make no difference whatever to this hardy creature—the man sat down on a half-crumbled fallen tree trunk, and gradually the stallion drew nearer. He was troubled by the presence of this unloved man, but, nevertheless, in that particular place, he, Sky Pilot, chose to graze, and since the man sat quietly, and merely talked in a gentle voice, there seemed no particular harm.

And so Terry Shawn sat shuddering in the damp cold and picked seed grass, and patiently offered it. It was scorned for a long time. At length, as he held forth a large and choice bunch, Sky Pilot turned away and stared up the mountain. The clouds had parted and blown clean away from the mountain head, streaming toward the west with a shifting of the wind, and all the summit of Mount Shannon was revealed, heavily coated with white except where the shadowy ravines made streaks of black. That expanse of dazzling brightness made Terry Shawn shudder more deeply than before; and then Sky Pilot turned deliberately, and without sign of fear took the seed grass from Shawn's hand!

It was done so suddenly that Terry Shawn could hardly believe that the thing had happened. Amazed and delighted, he stretched out the empty hand. Sky Pilot, eyes blazing with fear and curiosity and hatred, stretched his head in answer, sniffed at the naked hand, and then flung away in a wildly frightened gallop.

Much, much to do! Indeed, the outlaw felt that he had hardly put his foot on the bottom rung of the ladder, but this much at least had been accomplished—by the will of mysterious Shannon, he had led the horse by the mane; by his own patience and calm, he had induced Sky Pilot to take food from that same hand.

Well, much could be done, after that. A step at a time, little by little!

Somewhere he had heard the Chinese fable of the old woman who sat at the roadside grinding an iron pestle in an empty mortar. "What are you doing, mother?" "I am grinding the pestle down to make a needle—"

Patience would be its own reward, in that case, but here there was something profoundly more important—there was Sky Pilot!

Ah, let other men live as they would, with wealth and comfort around them, while he flashed through the wide Western ranges with such speed under him that cities and mountains and rivers would be spurned underfoot. With such a horse beneath him—with such a horse beneath him—!

So he soared in his imagination, like a wild-hearted boy, looking up from a fairy tale, flies through the sky from Al Raschid's Bagdad to Valhalla. He followed the stallion, but this time the chestnut made as if to charge him, and fled away across the meadow, squealing with rage.

Enough for that day; so he turned his back reluctantly on the horse and wandered over to the creek.

By now its waters were fallen still farther, and instead of the loud and solemn thunder with which it went down through the trees before, it had dropped to a quiet and melancholy singing, composed of a song of many notes.

Berry and Hack Thomas strolled down the bank toward him. He turned resolutely upon them.

"Jim and Hack," said he.

"He's pickin' up a little," said Hack Thomas. "He's findin' his vocabulary. What's ridin' you, kid?"

"I never should have dragged you two up here with me. I thought I'd take a little fling at the horse, and then call it quits. Well, boys, I find that the horse means a lot more to me than I had thought."

He waited. Jim Berry exclaimed, "Well, damn me, if I ever heard of a—"

"Aw, shut up," said Hack Thomas gently. "You do what you want to do, kid. It's your right. Stay right here till you get snowed in. If it's too deep for you to move, it's gunna be sort of hard for the sheriff to get at you, too. You'll have a snug winter, and you'll get to know the horse fine by the time that the spring thaws come around. Maybe you'll work up sign language with old Shannon, too!"

The irony of these remarks did not escape Terry Shawn, but he let the arrows fly without heeding them.

Before another remark could be made, Jim Berry exclaimed, "There he is! There he goes through the trees! On foot!"

And he reinforced his words by snatching

out a revolver and trying a pot shot. They heard the bullet go crackling through the branches, and a thin fall of leaves followed beneath its course.

"There's who?" asked Shawn.

"The kid—the one that chased us up the ravine. I seen him there, and by God, he's tracked us on foot this far! He wants blood!"

He pointed into the trees in the direction in which he had seen the stranger.

They were excited enough. Gun in hand, they scanned the trees and made their plans.

Big Hack Thomas and Berry would go down the creek and cut into the woods in the course of a hundred or so yards, trying to pick up the trail. Terry Shawn should move up the creek and enter softly, trying to cut off the advance of the enemy if he went in that direction.

He saw his two confederates slip down the creek, while he crossed to the farther bank and turned up in the opposite direction. He entered the trees where there was a narrow opening through a dense thicket. Behind this he came to a more open bit, through which he could look to a considerable distance. And here he took cover to watch and wait, for he felt reasonably sure that the youngster would skirmish up through the woods avoiding the thicket, because of the noise that must be made in pressing through it.

Now, lying prone between a pine and a birch, where he was sheltered by a tall, spare growth of grass, he scanned the trees before him steadily and all his senses grew gradually more and more alert.

He heard the whisper of the wind in the branches, a flutter of wings as a bird made off from a lofty perch, and then the singing of the creek in the near distance. Finally, there was the indubitable sound of a gun exploding, farther down the valley; it brought him half to his knees, but he sank back again.

One shot could hardly have begun and ended the battle. There would be a fusillade before the two men brought down that elusive and dangerous youngster with his accurate rifle; and certainly with one shot the latter could not have dropped the pair of them.

So he settled himself to his vigil again and had barely made himself alert and comfortable, when a low voice said behind him, "Hands up, Shawn!"

He jerked his head around; there stood the youth There was a bright gleam of his hair beneath the brim of his ridiculously huge hat, but that brim descended so low that all the face was in steep shadow; only the rounded lines of an absurdly youthful chin could be seen.

"Lie quiet," said the same low voice, "and take your hands away from that Colt!"

He did so, turned, and rose to his knees in spite of the leveled rifle—stood up—made a hesitant step forward—and then drew a great breath.

"Kitty!" cried Terry Shawn. "Kitty, in the name of God!"

31

"I DON'T KNOW whether it's me or my ghost," said Kitty with a twisted smile.

He took the rifle from her hands and the hat from her head so that her hair slipped out of the loose knot in which it was done and tipped down across her shoulders. It was so bright and rich that it seemed to cast a light upon her face.

"Lord God!" moaned Terry Shawn. "You

245

been ridin' along after me—*you* was the crazy kid!"

"Me? Crazy?" cried Kitty Bowen. "If I were a man," she added, "I'd never turn loose a gun on a man who'd had no warning!"

"Those were placed shots, Kitty—to turn you back, y'understand?"

"And then to shoot me when I wouldn't turn back?"

"No—aimed for the horse just to stop you!"

"Look!"

She pointed to a rent across the right knee of her trousers.

"That's where the bullet went on the way to the horse's heart! Oh, Terry, how could you kill her?"

"I didn't."

"Who?"

"I can't tell you that."

He never had seen a girl in such anger. He was amazed and mute.

"I'll tell you what," she said, "you *have* to tell me!"

"We wanted to stop you; wasn't it better to shoot at the horse than at the rider?"

"I wonder you didn't, Terry Shawn! Or is a girl too small a target?"

"How could I know it was you, Kitty?"

"You didn't much care."

She turned her back on him and hurried away, so that he had to run to place himself in front of her.

"Listen to me!" he begged.

"Don't touch me!"

"I ain't going to. But where are you going to go?"

"Home!"

"Will you only let me get you a horse and ride along with you?"

"I wish I'd never met you!" said she.

He was pale and tense as he listened.

"Most likely you do," said he.

He stared silently at her, lost in woe, tight-lipped with grief.

Then: "I don't believe you," he declared.

"I don't care what you believe," she answered.

Suddenly he stepped closer.

"Don't you touch me, Terry Shawn! I—I have a gun."

He brushed the rifle aside. It fell unregarded to the ground while he picked her up lightly in his arms and muffled her struggles and sat down with her on the crumbling top of a fallen log.

He waited, saying nothing; and because

the tears and the sobs came faster and faster, she pitched forward against his shoulder, shaking with her grief and excitement.

"You didn't want me!" cried Kitty through her tears. "You just tried to herd me away from you.

"Steady up! Steady up!" said he. "There's nothin' to shy at; it's all straight road; there's no trouble at head; and we're pointed home."

"You needn't talk to me as if I were a horse, Terry Shawn."

He was silent; the sobbing grew fainter; the body was less shaken by grief.

Then: "Oh, Terry!"

He waited, still cradling her, his heart aching with grief and with joy as the warmth of her body stole into him. In his strong hands, she seemed as slight as a boy, but wonderfully softer. He would take her back to her home and say to her father and mother, "Forgive me; I thought she was growed up; I didn't know she was only a baby, like this."

As the weeping ended she looked up and said, "You wouldn't send me back to 'em?"

"Me?" he echoed vaguely.

She caught the lapels of his coat and her eyes were wild.

"I'd kill myself, first!" she cried. "I wouldn't stand it. Terry, you're gunna keep me always with you—you'll promise me that!"

"God help me to do what's best!" he groaned.

Somehow the man's clothes accented her youth, her ignorance, her wild-hearted folly, and the more mightily he loved her, the more certainly he saw that he must save her from the wilderness and himself. He set his teeth.

32

WHEN JIM BERRY and Hack Thomas slipped cautiously out from the woods, having seen nothing as a trail in their portion of it, they were amazed to observe their quarry walking boldly ahead of them, rifle in hand, and Terry Shawn beside. They approached with speed and silence. Nevertheless, that catlike ear of Terry Shawn detected them, and turning he called, "I got him, boys!"

The slender form turned also. "Yes, he got me, boys!"

Hack Thomas stopped as one suddenly struck in the face; but Jim Berry lurched forward.

"It's Kitty!" he cried.

And she, equally excited, ran to meet him, took both his hands, laughed joyously up into his face.

"Jim, Jim—*where* have you been?"

Their answers crossed one another; they walked aimlessly up the meadow, side by side, stopping now and again with bursts of cheerful laughter. And Terry Shawn remained behind, scratching his chin. Hack Thomas joined him.

"There you are," said Hack. "That's the weak side of Jim. Now, you take a young gent like him, punch like a mule and don't know how to miss a shot, ready to fight ten wildcats and eat 'em up, but still he's got to have a weak side. I say it's too bad!"

"Weak?" echoed Shawn. "Why, it kind of appears to me like he's acting strong, here!"

"The girls can't help lovin' Jim," admitted Hack. "It's his handsome face and the bigness of him, you see."

"He's kept you out of double harness, maybe?" suggested Shawn curiously.

"Oh; damn him," said Hack Thomas,

suddenly rather red of face, "let him go. What difference does it make what he's done? Only, kid, you look after him, now. He's making a dead set at her! I've given you a fair warning!"

He said it so point-blank that Terry Shawn set his teeth and lengthened his stride as he hurried up the valley. Hack Thomas made no effort to follow so rapidly, for, contenting himself with falling to the rear, he smiled and chuckled softly to himself. He even rubbed his hands and laughed until his shoulders quaked.

"Now, Jimmy," he said aloud but to himself. "Now, Jimmy, you watch yourself pretty careful, old feller!"

Jim Berry had no apparent thought of watching over himself, however. When they reached the shack, he set about making himself busy preparing the girl a basin of hot water for washing, and a cup of hot coffee to brace her after her fatigue. And he piled the pine boughs of two beds one on top of the other and heaped it deep with softest skins, so that she could lie down and rest.

It made no difference that she declined the invitation but sat on the edge of the bed, her hands locked around her knees, perfectly cheerful and gay and chatty; for it seemed to be fixed in the mind of Mr. Berry that she was a languishing and exhausted poor creature who must be handled as wilting flowers are handled.

"I'm not going to fade, Jim," she said, "until time does it to me. Get away and take care of yourself—but I don't mind a dash of coffee, if you got some handy!"

He looked on her and sadly shook his head; then he turned with a sigh.

"You look kind of weak, Jim," said she.

"Letting you come here—I ought not to say anything," said Berry, "but I can't help busting out. What was Shawn thinking of?"

"Nothing. He didn't know that I was coming."

"He didn't?" Mr. Berry laughed gently and wisely.

"*Did* he think that I'd really trail along after him?" cried the girl, flushed with instant pride and anger. "Did he expect me to come trailing after him?"

"I'm not saying nothing," said Berry, with a most eloquent shrug of the shoulders. "Only—"

He bit his lips, as though to keep something hack.

"I got to know!" cried Kitty.

"How can I talk?" said he. "Only—by God—"

"He *did* think that I'd come. Oh!" cried she, and covered her crimsoned face.

He answered obliquely, speaking as a strong man should to a woman in distress, with a tenderly deepened voice.

"Don't you worry none. I'm gunna see you through this, Kitty. I'm gunna take charge of things! Don't you worry. You jus' lay back and rest a while!"

33

PLAINLY THE WEATHER was changing. The strong wind had fallen away, and the last remnant of the cloud mantle had been snatched from the head and shoulders of old Mount Shannon. When sunset came, the colors streamed up all across the sky tinting it deeply at the horizon and blending with a mysterious delicacy in the zenith. For the moment, there was no atmospheric depth, but it looked like a vast Chinese bowl of porcelain, polished, and with the blackness of the mountains and their fringings of magnificent trees stamped against the tender background.

It was below freezing point. There was no fireplace or hearth inside the shack, for that seemed to be a luxury to Shannon. Fire he would use for cookery alone, and even in midwinter he sat in his house wrapped heavily with skins, but with no artificial heat in the place; indeed, he was rarely inside, except to clean and stretch skins and to sleep.

However, this manner of living did not please Jim Berry, because, he said, one could not expose a delicately nurtured girl like Kitty Bowen to the evil damp and cold of that cabin. He would not have it!

"Stuff!" said Kitty. "I'm fat, and cold don't bother me!"

However, he insisted, and, by his direction and chiefly by his work, a great bonfire was built close to the door of the house, so that a flood of heat and brightness entered every part of the shack. Kitty had protested once; afterwards she luxuriated in the warmth and in the comfort.

Shannon came home in the midst of the preparations for dinner. Hack Thomas, that same morning, had shot a fat buck and brought in the carcass on his mighty shoulders; now that venison had been roasted in the Dutch oven, and when the iron lids were removed, through the still air stole a pervading fragrance, richer, to those hungry nostrils, than the fragrance of roses, more delightful than the pure odor of the pines.

Into that happy scene, at that lucky moment, came Shannon and greeted them solemnly with his raised hand and a charming smile. Then he saw the girl, and his smile went out. He scanned the group hastily and suddenly pointed to Jim Berry with a frown of scorn and anger. It was perfectly clear what he meant; and Berry with both hands presented the trouble to Terry Shawn. The latter was a man of steady nerves, but now he grew uneasy. The sparkling, angry eyes of this hermit subdued and troubled him.

"Look here, Shannon," said he. "I want to tell you how it is. You see, Miss Bowen, yonder—" He broke off with a terse, "Hell, he can't understand."

Shannon, however, seemed to master his first emotion of disgust and contempt. He approached the girl and raised his hat as he bowed before her, so that it seemed, for a moment, that words must come from, the speaking courtesy of his face.

Then he went on into the horse shed, with the beautiful chestnut following at his heels, and dancing and shying away from the proximity of the others.

Kitty, tears in her eyes, faced the others.

"Isn't there some way of telling him that I'm not bad?" she asked.

"He don't think you're bad," said Terry Shawn. "He heaps it all on me. Thanks, Jim!"

He turned to Jim Berry with a cold glance that bit in between the eyes of Berry and left his brain iced and numb with a sudden fear. However, he shook off that humor and bent his attention upon the girl.

After a silent meal Berry put the final touches on Kitty's sleeping place and then, in a gentle voice: "You're played out," he said to the girl. "You better turn in and have a long sleep; come along and I'll fix up a light for you."

He led the way into the shack and left Hack Thomas with the outlaw, alone.

"You been watching?" asked Hack Thomas, with quiet malice. "Seen how he's taken her in hand? Oh, he's smooth and he's deep!"

Terence Shawn made no reply; he was sunk in a deep and black reflection, and in his turn he went into the shack and rolled into his bed, while handsome Jim Berry came out to sit by the fire and his friend Hack.

They smoked in quiet, for a time.

"When'd you get to know her so well?" asked Thomas at the last.

"I used to work on their place," answered Jim Berry. "Used to ride Bowen's range, and I taught the girl how to handle a horse. She had the nerve of a regular bronc peeler, and a nacheral seat and pair of hands; so we got on. She was only a little kid, then, with a whip of pigtails hangin' down her back."

"She's come on, since then," suggested Hack Thomas.

"She's come on," agreed the lady's man.

"Tell me something," said Hack Thomas, pretending to yawn. "You ever hear from Lulu any more?"

"Who?"

"Lu Perkins."

"Oh, your old girl?"

"Maybe you could call her that," admitted Hack with carefully studied indifference.

"I ain't heard from her for a year," said Jim Berry. "Got tired of writing all the time. That girl, she'd write you a book; took an hour to read one of her letters. I chucked it; I got tired!"

Mr. Thomas was silent for a moment, and then he murmured, "You always get tired, kid. You always chuck them, pretty quick!"

"A man's gotta have variety," remarked Jim Berry. "Can't live on venison for a year; can't live on ice cream, either. I'm gunna turn in."

"Wait a minute!"

"Well?"

"I wanted just to ask you—you been watching the kid?"

"Kitty?"

"Shawn, I mean."

"What about him?"

"He's looking pretty black. If I was you, I'd keep my gun loose in the holster!"

The other exclaimed savagely, "I've let him come over me once, and I don't aim to let him try anything again. If he's wanting that girl—let him keep her! That's all I got to say. Let him keep her if he can. But if he wants another kind of trouble, I'm ready for him night or day, with a knife or a gun or any damn way that he says!"

"That's the way," said Hack Thomas dryly. "Talk right up, Jimmy. Don't you back up a step till you back right into your grave!"

Jim Berry shrugged his shoulders, grunted, and retreated toward his sleeping quarters.

34

HACK THOMAS HAD somewhat the nature of a politician. A politician, it may be taken, is one who controls without seeming to have the upper hand. A politician works from the inside; by means of a smile he does more than by means of a blow. So it was with Hack Thomas.

He never had forgotten pretty Lu and the days when he had hoped to make her his wife, for his rough ways of living brought him rarely in contact with women. She had fitted neatly into his mind; she was all that he hoped for and wanted; and Jim Berry had taken her away. For a month he had alternated between grief and rage, wondering whether or not he should go

to Berry, gun in hand, and demand satisfaction, but he and Berry had been partners
in crime for many years and a little delay
blunted the edge of his purpose, but never
removed his malice.

That anger which is unexpressed and
swallowed often enters the blood; at least,
so it did with Hack Thomas, and he had
waited through many a long month for the
chance to break even with his companion.
Now fortune had placed the chance in his
hands, and he worked with the opportunity
as he found it. If he had been asked directly
whether or not he wished the death of Terry
Shawn or of Jim Berry, beyond a doubt
he would have answered with some horror
that he had no such purpose. He was
merely giving a certain shaping and direction to events, and then they could take
care of themselves, for it is often the
politician's way to start forces in motion
for the mere pleasure of starting, letting
chance handle them, once under way.

Bitterness poisoned the heart of Hack
Thomas; he wanted the whip to be laid
upon the back of Jim Berry, wanted to see
him bleeding and broken, after which he
dimly visioned himself healing the wounds
and caring for the stricken man. Suppose

that the blow was one which could not be healed? Of that, he refused to think; and again like a politician, permitted himself only to look as far as the prospect proved agreeable.

The next morning saw indefatigable Jim Berry again at work to please and care for Kitty Bowen, while Shannon walked off hunting, and Hack lingered around the cabin with no care on his hands except to watch young Terry Shawn earnestly at work with the chestnut. It seemed to Hack Thomas that the youth was making little enough progress, but the patience of Shawn was like that of the Chinese exemplar which he had taken to heart.

Many small steps at last make a mile, so he worked over Sky Pilot with endless endurance. He had reached a point, now, where Sky Pilot accepted him as a necessary part of the landscape, even if not a pleasant one. He would graze to the very feet of Terry Shawn; he would take grain, with some snortings and precautionary starts and stampings, from the hand of the gun fighter. It seemed that Sky Pilot realized there was some sort of game which he and this man were playing together.

At least, he saw no harm in taking delicious tidbits from this fellow, or even in allowing his smooth neck to be stroked, eventually, while he reached for a tuft of seed grass.

Many a wise old mustang, a hardened veteran of the range, might have told him that familiarity with man is apt to breed loss of independence, and that by cunning kindness man breaks the spirit, as well as through the use of whip and spur and jaw-breaking curb, but there was no such warning for Sky Pilot.

He had in mind only one sort of man-fashioned danger, and that was the danger of spur and quirt and gripping cinches. So now he allowed this former enemy, this present smooth-voiced youngster, to while away the time with him, wandering idly about with him over the rich grass of the meadow, more like another horse than like a human being.

Jim Berry and the girl disappeared up the stream, fishing in the fallen waters; they returned barely before noon, there gay voices ringing as they laughed together; and as Berry went off to cut fresh evergreen boughs and resinous wood for the fire, Shawn came into the shack and met the girl.

She was cleaning fish like a good house-wife and preparing them for cooking; and Shawn stood over her and looked down with a melancholy interest on the flying, supple hands. Hack Thomas arose and wandered away toward the trees, perhaps to help Jim Berry, perhaps to mask his contented grin.

"Be useful, Terry," said the girl. "Bring me a bucket of water."

"Kitty," said he.

"Hurry."

"Kitty," he repeated, and she looked up at him.

"Now what's up? Have you got a tooth-ache, Terry? You've been glooming around something terrible."

He hooked his thumb over his shoulder.

"I want to talk to you about Berry."

"Go on, then."

"How long you known him?"

"About twenty times as long as I've known you. Why?"

"I only wanted to say that Berry has got a name, y'understand?"

She stood up.

"A name for what?"

"For having his way with the girls."

263

She paused, stared, and then exclaimed sharply, "Terry Shawn, I'm surprised!"

"Ask anybody," said Shawn. "Everybody knows!"

"To come here like this," said she, "and talk behind a man's back!"

His teeth clipped together with a sharp click.

"If you wanted to say something about him, why not talk out right in front of him?"

"I'm talking to you," said Terry Shawn, "because I have a right to talk. I don't want to see you making a fool of yourself over—"

"A fool of myself!" she cried. "Are you calling me a fool?"

"You've made up your mind to get hot," said Shawn sullenly. "There's no use me saying anything more, I suppose!"

"There's a lot of use," she cried, growing more and more angry. "You've accused poor Jim Berry when his back was turned. Just because he was polite. You might learn something from him, Terence Shawn!"

He regarded her sadly, without passion, and then turned slowly away.

"I'm not through. I have something more to say!" exclaimed Kitty Bowen.

He went back to her, grim of face.

"He's a quick worker," said Shawn bitterly. "It took him one evening and a morning to show you that I'm not worth bothering over. I gotta hand it to him. He's slick!"

"You—" said Kitty, trembling with shame and wrath. "Terence Shawn—there ain't a speck of shame in you."

"He'd be glad to hear us talk like this," said Terry Shawn. "Well, I'll tell you, Kitty. When he comes back from the woods, don't you let him go around about here with any wrong ideas about me. You tell him out and out what I think about him, will you?"

"Jim Berry is a gentleman!" said the girl hotly. "I never met a kinder, better, straighter, gentler—"

"Rat!" said Mr. Shawn. "You might tell him that's what I said he was. A rat. A low-down, sneakin', yaller rat. A gnawin', night-livin', worthless rat. When you're tellin' him the other things, you just speak up and tell him that I called him that. And when I come back here, I aim to expect that he'll know what I said!"

This last speech he delivered very slowly, haltingly, as though he were hunting for the proper words and was satisfied with

265

those which he found. It reduced Kitty Bowen to a frozen silence that held her while Mr. Shawn turned on his heel and sauntered down the meadow to the place where the shining chestnut was standing.

Then she seemed about to start after him, but at this point Jim Berry came out of the woods, heavily laden with pine boughs, and came up to the shack with his burden.

He dropped the boughs and looked keenly at her, her white face turned toward the distant and retreating form of her lover. The faintest of smiles appeared upon the lips of Jim Berry. He banished it at once, and said quietly:

"Is there anything wrong, Kitty? You look sort of upset!"

"Anything wrong?" cried the girl, clasping her hands.

"Everything's wrong, and something terrible is going to happen!"

"I hope not," murmured Jim Berry.

"He's going to fight," said Kitty Bowen. "I could see it in his face. He's going to fight—he'll—Jim, saddle your horse and ride away as fast as you can, because if he comes back here and finds you, he'll make trouble!"

Mr. Berry lost a great deal of color on the instant. He stared at the girl, and he stared at the far-off form of the gun fighter; instinctively he reached for a gun and froze his grip on the handles of it.

"What's happened?" he asked hoarsely.

"It's me," said Kitty ungrammatically. "He thinks that you've been paying too much attention to me—and he's in a passion—he's furious—he won't listen to reason! Go quickly, Jim. Otherwise something terrible will happen!"

Mr. Berry moistened his white lips. He was rather glad that the girl, instead of glancing at him, kept her frightened eyes still fixed on Terence Shawn in the lower meadow.

"I don't run away from no man," he said bravely.

At that, she turned sharply and suddenly on him.

"You don't mean that you'd stand up to Terry Shawn?"

"I mean that I won't be bullied!" said the stout Jim Berry. "Who's Shawn? I've met harder men than him. He can bully cowards—and he can bully women," added Jim Berry, laying his hand on her arm gently, "but he can't bully me!"

"Good heaven!" moaned Kitty Bowen. "If you stay—if you stay—"

She did not finish her sentence; it needed no finishing, as a matter of fact, and she turned back to stare apprehensively toward Shawn in the distance. Jim Berry, having made his proud boast, slipped around the corner of the house and into the horse shed.

35

MR. BERRY'S COURAGE was, of course, undoubted but it was of a peculiarly quiet type; it appeared only when he wanted to use it, and it might safely be said that his discretion was at least as great as his valor. He had been known to stand up to three armed men, but he knew the three men against whom he stood; on this occasion he also knew the man against whom it was proposed that he should stand, and, although he was certain that few men in all the world were more accurate than Jim Berry with a revolver or a rifle, he was sure that the young outlaw was among those few. Not for an instant did he intend to make his boast good, but when he got into the horse shed, he jerked his saddle from its hook and tossed it on the back of his horse.

Even as he saddled and bridled the mare, he was listening with a tense attention to all sounds outside of the shed, and when a step approached the door, he whirled about and waited with a drawn revolver and a set jaw. There might be some difference between his marksmanship and that of young Terence Shawn, but if Shawn came through a door at him, he would certainly wipe that difference out.

It was not Shawn. The broad shoulders of big Hack Thomas came through the door. With desperate haste, Jim Berry strove to put his revolver out of sight, but he was much too late. Hack had seen. He leaned one hand against the wall and smiled benevolently upon his old friend.

"Cutting and running, Jimmy?" he suggested.

"Why should I cut and run?" asked Jimmy.

The answer came with disheartening certainty, "Shawn!"

"And why should I have any trouble with that Shawn, will you tell me?"

"Sure I'll tell you. You been spending too much time with Terry's girl."

"Damn Terry, an' damn his girl!" replied the other savagely. "I wish that I'd never laid eyes on the pair of them!"

"Maybe—maybe!" answered big Thomas. "Only, kid, I'd like you to take notice—chuck Shawn and we chuck the biggest and the surest job that we ever tackled. Enough coin to retire on, I'd say!"

"Is he the only fightin' man in the world?" asked Berry, with heat and scorn and fear commingled.

"No, he ain't the best," said Hack Thomas. "He's only the best that I ever met up with or ever had anything to do with. He's twice as straight a shot and twice as quick as anybody I ever saw pull a gun. And we need him, kid."

"You've got him," answered Berry. "Well, take him along. If you can't replace him, you can replace me. Stand aside, Hack. I'm on my way!"

"Sonny, you're makin' a fool of yourself," replied the older of the two. "Throw your reins and climb down and talk common sense. How long we been workin' together, old son?"

"I dunno. What's that got to do with it?"

"We've teamed for near six years, ain't we?"

"About that. Hack, clear out of the doorway and let me through."

"Oh, back up!" exclaimed the other. "Kid, in those six years have we ever been in jail?"

"I don't suppose that we have."

"Can we ride through nearly any part of the range and pass as good, ordinary, honest cowpunchers?'

"I suppose that we can.

"Now, d'you think that I'm gunna chuck six years of luck even for the sake of a hell-fire gent like young Shawn?"

"I like what you say fine," answered Jim Berry. "Only there's this to say—am I to stay around here and get my head blowed off by Shawn?"

"That's straight and that's frank," replied the other. "The fact is, he'd kill you, Jimmy; you know it and I know it. But there's another fact—he's not going to get the chance!"

"What'll stop him?" asked Berry. "The swine is hot as fire, already. He wants my scalp and if he has a chance at me, he'll fill me full of lead."

"You could back up a little, Jim, knowing the stake that we're playing for!"

"Back up?" asked Berry, flushing dark. "I back up and let the girl see me taking water? No, I'll be damned if I will. No matter how I may feel, I've never took water before, and I'll never start taking it for any swine of a gun fighter that ever stepped on two legs. You write that down in red, Hack. What sort of a man d'you think I am?"

"I understand," said Hack Thomas.

He paused and considered.

"I'll be on my way, then," repeated Berry nervously.

"Hold up! Hold up!" commanded his older companion. "I'm going to see my way through this here and keep you and keep the kid, too. I want him: I got to have you. Now, old son, you know that I can manage things pretty good. Only tell me, first, if you really want to cut and go?"

"No! I never hated anything worse. Aside from leaving you, I throwed a bluff with the girl and if I go off now she'll write me down as a yellow dog. Only—it's better for me to quit now than it is for me to back up under the gun of the kid!"

"I tell you what—I'm going to handle

the kid, and you'll have no trouble out of him. That's the straight of it, my friend. I'll iron these things out."

"And if you fail to, then I'm simply a dead man. Is that right?"

"Not so certain. No gun fight ever is certain. You'd have one chance in four, even on an even break."

"Thanks," said Berry. "It ain't the kind of odds that I play!"

"Well," answered Thomas, "tell me this. Could he beat the pair of us, then?"

"The pair of us?"

"Kid," cried Hack Thomas, "don't you understand? The minute that the pinch comes and he starts an actual gun fight with you, I'll be at him. He won't be expecting me. I'll shoot Mr. Terry Shawn into hell before he has a chance to get his guns out. Will you trust me?"

Jim Berry listened with staring eyes. "D'you mean that?" he asked huskily.

"I mean that, son!"

"It'd save my face before the girl," commented Mr. Berry. "And give me your hand, Hack. You always had the head for everything!"

"Leave it all to me," said Hack, with the air of a commander addressing his officers before action. "All you got to do is to pipe down small and not kill yourself bein' nice to the girl. I guess that you've had a little lesson out of this, Jim?"

Jim Berry mopped his forehead; he needed to make no other rejoinder.

"You'll be keeping out of the way of the girls that other fellows have staked out, after this," went on Hack Thomas with more sternness than before, "and if you do that, you'll be keeping out of trouble. Now, kid, listen to me. Shawn ain't a bully. He won't press too far, and if he just sees that you ain't bothering the girl no more, he'll be contented. I can have a few words with him; I'll smooth things over fine. Don't you worry a bit."

"And if you *don't* smooth things over?"

"I've told you what I'll do in that case. I'll fill the kid full of lead the minute that he starts to make a play at you."

"Good old man!" sighed Berry, and moisture appeared in his eyes, as though he were overwhelmed by the goodness of his companion.

So they arranged the thing, and Jim Berry, left alone in the shed, slowly stripped saddle and bridle from his horse. He made many pauses, for he was still far from sure that he was following the wisest course.

At last, however, the thing was done, and he stepped from the shed into the open. He walked slowly; gravity was in his face; gravity was in his heart, and he felt that the entire world had changed.

Certainly the atmosphere in the valley had altered, for now the bright sun which had been so brilliant was gone, and in its place there was again the stealing, chilling mist of gray, growing momently thicker. It seemed to be breathed forth from the trees, for they already were massed solidly with it, and the lower meadow was clouding over, so that Terence Shawn and the young stallion were well-nigh lost to view, though big Hack Thomas, as he strode toward them, could be made out plainly.

At the edge of the shack, Jim Berry glanced earnestly after them.

Kitty Bowen, on her knees working up the fire in the oven, said to him:

"You've sent Hack out to make peace, Jim?"

"What makes you think that?" he asked.

"You don't need to be ashamed," said the girl gravely.

"To turn an ordinary fellow against Terry

is like turning in a wolf against a tiger; Well, I hope that Hack has luck, but I'll tell you what—"

"Go on."

"If I were you, I'd back up, I'd saddle my horse, and I'd slide out of the valley!"

He looked calmly on her. His courage was returning, he even could smile.

"I never back up, Kitty," said he. "You ought to know that. And I'm too old to start learning."

"Ah," cried Kitty, rising to her feet, "maybe it'll turn out all right, after all!"

"What makes you think that?"

"Look! Now that he's done that, he won't care for anything, he'll be so happy!

She had pointed, and out of the white and stealing mist, Berry saw Shawn coming toward them, leading the stallion easily along, his hand on top of the chestnut's neck.

36

IN FACT, ALL the danger which lay before them was forgotten by Jim Berry in the bewilderment with which he stared toward the outlaw and the horse which walked beside him. It raised Terry Shawn to a different plane and altered him from his old self, just as an eagle penned with clipped wings is altered when the wing feathers have grown. So it seemed with Shawn, as he walked by the side of the half-tamed horse, that wings had been given to him, and awe fell upon the watchers.

Hack Thomas, striding at the side of the youngster, had more in mind than the subduing of a wild horse. Nevertheless, he could not help being filled with admiration, as if he had seen some miracle performed that left his eyes starting and his forehead hot. He knew the record of Sky Pilot, and that record was worth commenting upon in all the rough camps of men up and down the range. Yet here was Sky Pilot, literally in the hand of a human enemy!

The chestnut walked jauntily at the side of the outlaw, not in the fashion of one who has to go, but rather out of his free will, content in the knowledge that he could leave at his own volition whenever he chose. Now and again, he paused a little, and sometimes he would turn his lordly head and stare into the distance toward the white crags of the upper mountain; and sometimes he would turn and nose the man who walked beside him. It was strangely as though he were being drawn between a contempt of all things human and a love of the wildness on the one hand, and on the other the love of man above all else.

"How'd you do it, kid?" asked big Hack Thomas in a rather hoarse voice.

"Shut up and leave him alone, will you?" asked Shawn nervously. "Don't you see him tremble when you speak? I haven't got him—I've only got a fingertip on him; I'm hangin' by an eyelash!"

Yet, unquestionably, he had passed the divide between enmity and friendship, and the chestnut trusted him, or had begun to trust him. He paused, and Sky Pilot walked on, but he walked in a circle and came back to this new human acquaintance. Terry Shawn, much moved, rubbed the horse's nose and stroked his neck.

"It's like I'd opened a door and stepped inside the house," said Shawn, half to the horse and half to Thomas. "I've hung my saddle and bridle on the peg and I'm gettin' hospitality. My God, my God, Hack, what's the good of whips and spurs when a little time and conversation will give you a horse like this? You hear me talk? I'll never again break a horse with floggings and the spurs. I'll break 'em with an open hand!"

"It'll cost you thousands of dollars' worth of time," said Hack Thomas.

"It'll give me millions in another way," answered the youth.

"Well, tell me how?"

"What is the difference between a friend and a hired man?" asked Shawn.

And Thomas was silent. At last he said, "They ain't all like the stallion, there.

"A poor friend," said Terry Shawn, with infinite conviction, "is better than the best of hired men. Run along with you, Sky Pilot!"

He clapped his hands and waved them, at which the stallion flaunted away, tossing his heels in the air and snorting.

"You've lost him, you fool!" cried Hack Thomas.

"You watch and see. D'you think that he don't know the difference between that and the crack of a whip? Aw, he knows, well enough. Watch that!"

The chestnut had circled the meadow like a flash of red silk, and now he drew up well ahead of Shawn, his head high, his feet planted wide, his eyes flashing, for all the world like a playful child ready for a game.

"Get out, you scoundrel!" yelled Shawn, and leaped forward, his fist thrown up.

Sky Pilot reared, smashed at the turf with his descending hoofs, and backed away; another lunge, and he squealed in answer and, flinging himself into the air, bucked and cavorted in such a way that the most cunning of jockeys could not have kept a seat on him for ten seconds.

"He's gone amok again!" shouted Hack Thomas. "Look at the devil! Oh, Terry, you blockhead, you've broken the charm!"

Terence Shawn merely laughed, and, stepping forward with outstretched hand, in another moment his arm was around the neck of the stallion and leading him along passively enough.

"I've got him by more than a fingerhold," said Terence Shawn, exulting. "I've got him by a lot more than that, and, God willing, Hack, I'll make him mine forever!"

"What'll the greaser say to that?"

"He had him," said Shawn grimly, "and he chucked him away. He had him and couldn't own him. He's lost his chance!"

"And what about old man Shannon, then? He didn't chuck his opportunity?"

For answer, Terry Shawn scowled savagely and spoke not a word; so that Thomas shrugged his shoulders and smiled a little. It was plain that he had quickly reached the end of the rope of Shawn's integrity. For that matter, Thomas did not wonder at it; he himself would have paid much good coin of the realm to stand in relation to the stallion as Shawn did.

However, he added after a moment, "You can take the horse, I suppose, and get away with it: All the same, there may be trouble."

"What kind of trouble?" asked Shawn sourly.

"I mean," answered Thomas, "that the best man most usually wins, in any sort of a game."

"And Shannon is the strongest man in this here valley?" challenged the boy.

"Wait and see. He's the strongest man here; we're in the hollow of his old hands; I've always felt it since I first laid eyes on him. Hey, what hell is popping up yonder?"

He pointed.

All the lofty head of Mount Shannon had lain naked and crystal white, a moment before, but now it was abruptly changed, for with a wind rushing out of the north the familiar mantle of clouds was being flung around the shoulders of the giant. It looked like a vast explosion, as though the center of the mountain were being rent, and the smoke and fury of the convulsion were escaping through the cleft ribs of the monster and ascending the sky. Wide-flung on either side, the mantling clouds streamed upwards, and in another moment the summit of Shannon was crowded with gigantic confusion. long arms of shadow were seen reaching down the ravines, and then the clouds began to fling out faster and faster from the summit, snapping off from the main cloud masses, and sailing in frantic haste across the southern sky.

"What hell has broke loose up there?" asked Thomas, again.

"It's winter," answered the youngster. "That's the first storm. We may have a white valley here before many hours, old son! But hell has certainly busted loose, yonder!"

"I hope that it busts loose no other place," remarked Mr, Thomas with sudden meaning.

"What other place do you mean?"

"Here in this here valley!"

"I dunno that I follow you, Hack."

"Kid," said the older man, "I know you

fine, and I know when you mean trouble; if you ain't got trouble in your eye right now, I'll eat my hat. Who is it for? Berry?"

"I've said nothing about Berry," returned Shawn darkly.

"I've said nothing about Berry," mimicked the other.

"You don't have to say; you look the part. You're gunna bust loose, roaring like the wind up yonder—listen!"

As they paused and raised their heads, they could hear it plainly enough. It seemed at first to come from the trees; then out of the very ground at their feet the noise seemed rising. It was a deep note like thunder, but unbroken, like thunder, and with a weird, high, complaining falsetto note running through it, as though something tender and feminine were suffering under the hands of a roaring giant. Both of the men had heard that noise before, though never quite so clearly as in the sounding box of this ravine: it was the sound of the storm which was shooting through the upper regions of the air, and sending the echo of its bellowing along the mountainside.

"Hell's popping," said Thomas, apparently overawed, and his voice sinking as he spoke. "Look yonder, kid. There's the ghosts rising, when the magician hollers to them!"

He pointed. Toward the south, the white and low-lying mists which had been crawling thick and thicker into the woods now began to stream upwards, rising like long, white-draped arms toward the upper sky. Presently they seemed to touch the invisible force that flew through the middle air, and were snatched away bodily. Other arms rose, more and more rapidly; in a trice the whole body of the clinging mist had been snatched away, and the woods lay sullenly but nakedly revealed down the slope of the mountain.

"Something is gunna happen," said Hack Thomas grimly. "I can feel it. These here are signs! And it looks like he was the gent that sent them!"

He indicated old Shannon, who was striding from the edge of the woods with the carcass of a young deer slung across his shoulders. He came with great strides, and, whether it was his presence and the gray length of his beard, or the infernal commotion in the sky above them, it did seem for the moment that he was larger than human and more formidable. The two regarded him with awe.

"Now, kid," said Hack Thomas, reverting to his former subject, "I see that we're all fixed up. You got your horse just about in hand; and there's the job waiting for us down yonder in the plains. Do we start tomorrow morning, or this evening? Or are you gunna insist on raising hell with Jim Berry?"

The other looked curiously at him.

"What makes you think that I want to raise hell with Jim Berry?" he asked. "You started in warning me about him; now you talk small about him. What's the idea?"

"He's had his lesson," said Thomas eagerly. "He's scared to death, old son. He knows what he's headed for, now!"

"He's had his lesson?" repeated the other, with a burst of white anger. "His lesson ain't started, even! It's too late, I tell you. It's miles too late!"

37

THIS TOUCH OF temper made Mr. Thomas, in turn, grow very gray. He closed with

Terry Shawn and laid a heavy hand on his shoulder.

"Listen to me, kid," he murmured. "You feel kind of hard against Jim."

"Never mind what I feel."

"Lemme tell you something. Jim is scared to death. He sees what he's done, and he hopes that it ain't too late! Matter of fact, kid, I've had a hard job to keep him from clearing out of the camp."

"Why did he want to go?"

"Because of you. Berry's game enough; but he don't want to commit suicide. You hear?"

"I don't get what you drive at," exclaimed the youngster with a burst of impatience. "First you steer me at Berry, and point out that he's apt to turn the head of a girl. Afterwards—" he paused. Then he continued, "Afterwards you come around and tell me that Berry's sorry. Well, Thomas, I dunno that that's much good to me. Suppose that somebody picks your pocket and throws your purse away. Are you gunna let him say that he's sorry, and call it quits? Or are you gunna jail him?"

"Of course I see what you mean," replied Hack Thomas. "I see what you're driving at. You think that Jim Berry has made a great head with the girl. You think that they're pretty thick, eh? Lemme tell you, kid, that he means nothin' in her young life. Nothin' at all. He was handy and useful; he stood around smilin', and she just smiled back a little; that's all!"

"Did she send you over here to tell me this line of chatter?" asked the gunman, dropping his face a little and looking grimly through his brows at the other.

"She sent me nowhere at all. It's just because I like you, Terry, that I'm tryin' to stave off any trouble. I like you and I like Berry. So will you, when you get a better chance to know him."

"Study your horse when he's tired and your men when you're in a pinch," said Shawn. "I guess that I know him fairly well!"

"Not a mite. But whether you know him or not, whether you got hell in for him or not, you need money and you need big money, old son.

"What makes you say that?"

"Can you settle down with a girl like that without a stake?" inquired the other.

Terry Shawn's face blackened.

"We're not settling down," he said savagely. "Besides, I've talked enough."

Hack Thomas saw the youth stride past him, and in his fury at the sense that he had touched on the wrong topic at last, he gritted his teeth and drove his sharp heel into the turf. Then he hurried after and laid a restraining hand on Shawn's arm,

"Kid," he said, "will you listen to this? Is it better to kill Jim Berry now and lose about fifty thousand beans, or it is better to wait till you got the money in your pocket? Answer me that, will you?"

Shawn hesitated, growing sullen. "I dunno," he muttered at last. Then he flung out, in an agony rather than a rage, "I dunno much about anything, Hack. All I know is that I'm in hell. I've lost everything; I got nothing left. I used to have a thousand friends, like old Joe. Well, I chucked them, it seemed, for the sake of a girl. And then I've lost the girl. Everything has gone wrong. I've had her taken out of my hands. Aw, I ain't howling to have her back; I don't ask for charity; only I say that there ain't anything straight before me that's worth looking at except the chestnut stallion. Look at him! He's all that I got! And what's he good for? Simply to take me into one patch of hell and out again faster than the eye can follow. That's all that he's good for!"

His manner, however, denied these words, for as he spoke he dropped his head against the muscular cheek of the stallion, and Sky Pilot pricked his ears and stood like a rock. Hack Thomas, really moved, saw that it was a time to waste few words, and he merely said, "I leave it with you to act like a sensible fellow, old-timer. I say that you're wrong, what you think about the girl; and she's for you as much as ever. That's all. But she's gay; she's good-natured; she likes to be jolly; she wants to chatter a bit; and Jim Berry has been doin' all of those things. I only ask you this—watch him tonight, and see how he acts. If he wastes much time around her, then call me a liar and a fool! Son, he's going to keep hands off!"

"Because he don't want her," suggested the bitter Shawn. "Because he's tired of her already—"

He writhed at the thought, while Hack Thomas, seeing that words of no sort would now avail him, walked slowly ahead. He passed Shannon coming in with the deer, and for lack of anything better to do, or perhaps to show his respect for that grave-faced hunter, he took the burden from the strong old shoulders and carried it on toward the fire.

Shannon turned off and went toward Shawn, and the chestnut whirled away from its new friend and raced joyously toward the old one. The hermit waved it aside, and, pausing in front of Terry Shawn, he nodded to the stallion and then smiled with the utmost cheerfulness and kindness on the outlaw. After that, he went on, but this brief instant of meeting impressed Shawn more than the longest of speeches would have done, for it seemed to say, "I welcome you, my friend, in the companionship of the chestnut. You and I now are of one world, in a measure. Good luck be with you!" So he had to interpret Shannon's smile, coming at the very moment when he would have suspected something just the opposite, jealousy and hatred for having stolen some share of the affection and the trust of Sky Pilot.

So Terry Shawn, almost forgetting the girl and Jim Berry, lingered by himself and communed with such a portion of his nature as never before had looked back to him, eye to eye. Call it the higher self, or the inner mind, or the voice of conscience and its bright, resistless face; whatever it was, that instant of meeting with Shannon had altered life for Terry Shawn.

He remained alone with the new idea —hardly an idea, but rather a form as vague as the mist which lately had lifted from the trees; and, thinking of that, he raised his face to the cloud masses which were streaming through the upper sky. Not so high up, they seemed now, but sweeping lower and lower, brushing down toward the earth while the booming echo of the storm rolled faintly and terribly through the cañon. The head of Mount Shannon was quite lost in the northern storm, now, except for a single dim glimpse, now and then, as the very fury of the wind lifted the cloud screen for an instant. Such a glimpse he had now, incalculable masses of cloud and darkness being cleft and rolled apart, while the solemn face of the peak looked forth again.

And it seemed to Shawn that so it was with the man he had just met—silence and gentleness ruled his life, but in his breast there were mighty emotions, cast on a greater scale than those which could be lodged in the breasts of most men, just as the form and the features of Mount

Shannon were vaster than those of all the surrounding summits. Here in this cañon, living in this little shack, there was a regal and extraordinary presence, and Terry Shawn was overwhelmed by it.

If it brought more solemnly beautiful ideas of life to him, it brought also a sense of fear and of loss; for one thing, his own strength which always had seemed so great now seemed a petty matter, and the possession of the horse was gone from him and turned back to the hermit. Whatever the coin which Shannon had paid for Sky Pilot, the youth felt that he sighed as he thought of it.

However, there was a time for such reflections—not this present moment. He went on toward the house, slowly, head hanging a little; at least one thing had been gained, for, whereas a moment before all his thoughts had been turning toward big Jim Berry and a crushing vengeance, now Berry and vengeance seemed paltry things; and so was Kitty Bowen; so was Terry Shawn. Such had been the flash of divine light and kindness that had shone on the gun fighter that he began to understand, though dimly, the possibilities of a greater life and a wider mind. He breathed un-

292

easily; so great became the commotion in his mind that all the turbulence of the upper sky fell away in his eyes and was hardly worthy to be regarded.

In the lee of the house he sat down cross-legged and looked down the ravine with eyes that saw nothing of the coming of the storm; neither did he regard Kitty Bowen close by him, nor Jim Berry, quietly at work in the repair of his bridle, nor Hack Thomas singing in the horse shed, nor old Shannon cleaning a pelt.

But there was a pause in all work, from time to time, and all eyes turned up to the sky, for it was now plain that the storm would never stop until it had scourged the cañon through all its length. Just above their heads the clouds were pouring, rolling wildly, heaving, and leaping like creatures of an animate will, and now and again the smoky arm of the storm reached down to the shack and shook it from top to bottom and made the very ground tremble.

In the same manner, those arms of fury reached down into the woods, and when-ever that happened the listeners would hear crashings and batterings, and sometimes the loud screech of boughs ground mortally against one another. All the leaves which had been hanging to the trees—slowly turning russet or gold, pencilings of purple and yellow streaks, and blood-red torrents through the underbrush—all of these leaves now were stripped away wherever the storm wind reached down among them. Whereas the ravine had been a flowing tide of color, now they could pick out spots which suddenly had been harvested of all richness and left barren and brown.

Even Kitty Bowen paid some attention to this vast battle. In all the world there were few more even-minded and serenely practical persons than Kitty, but now she left the cookery with which she had been filling her hands all the day, and, standing by the corner of the shack, she faced the downward torrent of the storm.

38

THE STORM WIND which had been flooding just above the top of the house now lifted, shunted higher, perhaps, by some twisting of the wind currents as they gushed through the mountain passes; so streams of water from two firehoses meet in air and make a vast white flower of spray blossom in the middle air, and now as the countercurrents of the storm crushed their shoulders together in leaping around Mount Shannon, the whole sky began to boil; clouds were born and dissolved momently, and a vast riot raged over Shannon Peak.

However, this was a thing to be seen rather than heard, for the small group of people in the shack or around it were aware only occasionally of faraway screamings and moanings indescribably terrible or sad; otherwise, they were relieved from that burden of noise and they could speak again, but first they looked covertly at one another as though half expecting to find that something had been added or taken from their companions by the coming of that great storm. There is something expectant in the pause of a storm or an interlude in a cannonade; the nerves remain tensed and the mind teaches out for something to fill the void.

So Terence Shawn left his broodings about God, nature and himself and turned suddenly to the grim facts which had been in his mind before. There was Kitty Bowen who once had loved him; there was Jim Berry who, he felt had stolen her away; and here at Terence Shawn with idle hands!

He looked down at those bony, strong hands in amazement, as though they were capable of answering his question about their idleness; then he began to scrutinize the girl and Berry more carefully.

So darkly hooded was the sky that even in the full day there was as much light from the fire as from the heavens, and as Kitty Bowen worked in a rosy glow she seemed permanently stained, for when she turned from the fire, there still was color on her face and hands. She appeared to be totally absorbed in her cookery, but now and again, cautiously, she cast a sideglance toward Shawn, a clever, measuring look, as though she were estimating something about him. It angered him intensely; he felt like springing to his feet and crying, "You don't know me! You've never seen me in action, really, but you're going to see me soon!"

What was in her mind? Cold dislike, no doubt, contempt and scorn because he would not raise his hand against Jim Berry.

As for Berry, sedulously he avoided the eye of young Terry. It was true that he did not pour his offers of assistance upon the girl, now, and in this respect it might seem that he was striving to avoid giving further offense to Shawn, but, as the latter felt, there is no use in insulting a loser and it was plain in his mind that the tall and handsome fellow already had won. Now he rested upon his oars, so to speak, and would not look behind him.

Anger piled high in the mind of Terry Shawn, like cloud on cloud in the sky. In the meantime, big Hack Thomas was making a little idle conversation.

"We're going to get it pretty quick," he declared. "The old wind has done a little retreat, but pretty soon it'll come again and swamp the whole doggone valley. It's gunna be full of snow when it comes, too! You mark what I say, there'll be hell popping around here pretty soon, I guess!"

And he looked anxiously up to the overmassed heavens above them.

Suddenly Shawn stood up, stretched himself with care, as though to make sure that every muscle was in smoothest working order, and then turned to Jim Berry.

"Jim, I want to talk to you.

Jim Berry nodded, without glancing back.

"All right. Go ahead."

"It's private talk," said Shawn. "Just

come away from the shack with me, will you?"

He saw Berry stiffen a little; he saw Kitty Bowen catch her hands suddenly together, almost as though she had burned herself at the fire. And that maddened him; but he told himself that this was a plain token that she was cold with anxiety about the welfare of her new lover.

"I don't see any reason," said Jim Berry, speaking slowly and thereby retaining control of his voice, "I don't see any reason why you can't talk right here, kid."

"I'll tell you the reasons later on," Shawn assured him.

But Berry would not move.

"We'll have the wind smashing around the shack in another minute or two," said he. "Why not keep here in cover?"

"Berry," said the other solemnly, "what I got to say ain't the sort of a thing a woman should hear. You understand what I mean?"

Berry, before he answered, cast one eager glance at Hack Thomas, asking a volume of questions in one brief instant; and in return, he had a sullen nod from Thomas, who was biting his lip in the background.

Kitty Bowen sprang to her feet.

"Jim," she said, "don't you go a step away with him. I know what he wants!"

"You're a mind reader, maybe," said Shawn with bitterness. "What do I want?"

"You want trouble," she answered, "You want to fight because you think—well, we all know what you think!"

He was badgered to the last limit of indiscretion.

"You all know," said he, "so I'll say it out loud. Berry has cut the ground from under my feet; he's made his set at me, and he's won out. Well, that's all right. He can have you; I don't want a girl who changes quicker'n the wind; but because he's played low with a partner and played the sneak with me when I trusted him, him and me have got to settle our little account. Berry, will you come out here with me? And God help one of us!"

It was odd to see the change that came over him as he spoke, for up to this time he had appeared the least significant person in that camp, not to be matched, certainly, against the mysterious grandeur of old Shannon, or against the lofty stature and good looks of Hack Thomas and Berry; but now he had altered, and just as some downheaded undersized pony, which has passed unregarded in the pasture, steps on the track with sudden fire in its eye and the manner of an emperor, so Shawn stood before them, now, burning with anger and terrible as flame.

Had he been totally unknown to them, still he would have commanded their attention and inspired fear; but he was known well to them all, and the record of his wild achievements stood behind him like flickering ghosts of the men who had fallen before him.

Both Thomas and Berry were frozen in their places, but Kitty Bowen stepped straight before Shawn and caught him by the sleeves of his coat.

"Terry, dear," said she, "are you goin' to listen to reason for a minute?"

"'Terry—dear!'" he mocked her furiously. "Hell, girl, I know that I'm nothing to you, and I wish to God that you were nothing to me; but whatever you are, you can't make a blind bull of me and twist me around your finger. Will you stand back? Will you keep out of this?"

"I won't move," said Kitty, trembling and breathing deep. "I'm going to make you see what a—"

She could get no further, for Shawn

picked her up suddenly and lightly and placed her inside the door of the shack, which he slammed, and thrust home the bolt on the outside. There was a cry, and then a literal scream from inside.

"Terry, Terry! Let me out! You've been all wrong. I love you Terry! Don't hurt Jim Berry—he's done no wrong—he—"

She could not have spoken more foolishly, for her words seemed a headlong appeal not for the sake of Shawn but for the sake of Berry.

So the outlaw turned on his two companions, and a cold and terrible smile touched his lips.

"You—Berry," he gasped, "are you ready?"

"I'm ready," said Jim Berry grimly. "Mind you—you're wrong. But I won't back down. You've gone a long ways, kid, and you've raised your share of hell, but you've come to the end of your rope. I'm gunna blow the hell right out of you, Terry. You go for your gun."

"Me go for my gun?" sneered Terence Shawn. "I'm gunna kill you, Berry; and I'd kill you if I started with my back turned to you. I give you a flying start. Begin it, Berry!"

The glance of Jim Berry flickered ever so slightly toward Hack Thomas, and there was an imperceptible nod from that grim-faced fellow. Matters were not going as Hack had wished to have them go, but he was not fool enough to try protests at a time like this. The game had gone too far for retreat, and he knew it. There was only one choice, as it appeared to him, and that was between the two who were about to fight—should Berry or Shawn live? That question he had answered for himself long before.

"I'll never begin it," said Jim Berry sullenly. A little convulsion of nervousness twisted his mouth into a grimace, and he flushed hot with shame at this betrayal of his state of mind. "I'll finish, but I won't start."

"Stand over there, Hack," commanded Terry Shawn. "Stand over there and drop your handkerchief for us, will you? That'll do as a signal.

A great noise of battering began inside the shack; doubtless it was old Shannon trying to smash down the door, and the wild, sobbing voice of the girl went shrilling out to them; it was a mere tangle of words with little meaning, and that voice was lost completely, a moment later, and the battering against the door made to seem small and far off, by the final attack of the storm It had piled its airy mountains all around Shannon Peak and filled the whole northern skies with its towers which now began to topple and pour down the southern face of the great peak. Roarings and shoutings filled the ravine; the last words Shawn had spoken were empty mouthings as the huge wall of sound washed over them.

The blast of the wind struck Terry Shawn so violently that he was sent staggering before it, and that stagger saved his life. Jim Berry, persisting in his policy of nonaggression, had not touched his weapons, but Hack Thomas had made a quick draw, seeing that the final moment had come; the bullet was well aimed, but as he pulled the trigger the storm knocked Shawn before it, his foot caught in a root that arched above the surface of the grass, and he pitched forward on his face.

39

THERE IS A saying, not wholly authenticated, unfortunately, that when Wild Bill the Great was shot through the brain from behind and fell forward on the card table dead, he made his draw while he was falling. Certainly he was dead the instant the bullet touched him, and his hands were empty except for his cards, but when they picked him up, they found a heavy revolver clutched in either hand. The last contraction of muscles, the last instinctive message that quivered down the nerves, had made the dead man draw and prepare for battle.

It was less miraculous, then, that Terence Shawn was able to equip himself with two Colts in the very instant when he was dropping to the ground; but it was wonderful indeed that before his body actually struck the ground, his guns had spoken. One bullet went wild past the ear of Jim Berry; but the shot from his left hand struck Hack Thomas in the thigh, and he collapsed suddenly upon the ground.

Jim Berry had made his draw. He stood like an old-fashioned duelist, his left hand behind the small of his back, his side turned to the foe, and a barking revolver in his right hand. His first shot kicked a shower of dirt into Shawn's face, half blinding him. His second surely would have ended the days of Shawn, but the impetus of the outlaw's fall was not ended at once, and he tumbled twice over on his side, still pumping bullets from both guns as he rolled.

A man lying on the ground, as soldiers know, makes an ugly and difficult target; poor Jim Berry had a prone and rolling figure and he did very well with it. He chipped the toe of Shawn's left boot and he split-over the face of his coat just over the heart, but the luck was against him.

Shawn, coming to the end of his roll from his fall, steadied himself to drive home the final bullets, only to find that both his enemies were down, both had lost their guns in their falls, and both were groaning and cursing savagely.

With cautious guns balanced in his hands, Shawn rose just as the door of the cabin was burst open and Kitty slipped out before old Shannon. She ran at Terry like a fury, and, crying, "Give me those guns— oh, you murderer!—" she wrenched the weapons out of his nerveless hands and ran to where Jim Berry lay.

That, said Shawn to himself, was the certain proof that she loved the fellow. She was holding his head in her arms and calling out to him, and the mad surging of the storm cut away her voice at her lips.

Old Shannon was with them, however; and with his aid Terry carried both his victims into the shack. There the howling of the wind was kept away behind the stout log walls, and it was at least possible to attempt conversation.

Thomas had been hit only once; but Jim Berry was fairly peppered. A bullet had clipped through the calf of his left leg and another had torn his right arm from wrist to elbow, a deep and dangerously bleeding wound. The third was the most dangerous. For the slug had passed through both legs above the knees, and from the left leg there was a rhythmic spurting that told a serious tale of a cut artery.

As for Thomas, the bullet, flying on an upward course, had entered the thigh just above the knee, twisted around the bone, and come out through the buttock. He lay stiff with pain, bleeding terribly, but making no complaint.

When Shannon went to him, he knocked the hermit's hand aside and pointed imperiously toward Jim Berry. When Kitty Bowen hurried over to him, he shook his head.

"Save Jim," said he. "I've only got what's coming to me—"

She merely fell to work on him silently, her face white and tense, her hands sure as steel. She cut down the leg of the trouser and exposed the entrance wound, pumping steadily, and she gripped the thick muscles above it to cut off the flow.

"Quick, Terry! We got to have a tourniquet here! He'll be losing too much blood—"

"I can't leave Jim," answered the outlaw. "If only the old man could be some help with Hack—"

It was literally as though Shannon understood what was said. He turned back to Thomas again, and he fell to work with perfect calm and method to make two powerful tourniquets to stop the flow of the blood.

But it was nasty work; the floor of the cabin began to look like the floor of a shambles; there was little said and hardly a sound from anyone except now and again a deep, muttering groan from one of the wounded.

So they worked fiercely, and as they toiled the storm freshened and rose from one impossible crescendo to another until the wild bellowing voices roared back and forth across the echoing valley with a continual booming.

For two long hours, patiently and carefully they worked, and at the end of that time the wounded men lay in some comfort, still tightlipped with pain but braced with some heavy drains from brandy flasks.

"Terry," said Hack Thomas at the last, "God knows that I got no right to speak to you or any other honest man, but the fact is that Jim and me are partners. I couldn't see him tackle you alone. And even with the two of us fighting, and me taking the jump on you, this is the way that it turned out!"

"I don't blame you much," replied Shawn gently. "I know that some men figure different from others; he was your partner and you had to stand by him; well, you had your own way of doing that. And here's the end of this game for me, boys. I'm saying goodbye. Jim, there's my hand; and I wish you better luck with her than I've had. So long."

He shook hands with Berry, wrung the hand of old Shannon, and then stepped to the door. There was no word from him to the girl, nor so much as a glance at her, and she stood with downcast head in the corner. The force of the wind was falling rapidly, but still it howled wildly enough to give much point to what Berry said when he cried, "Man, you'll be froze in one hour, if you go out into that storm!"

"I've seen as bad before," said Shawn. "It don't worry me, Jim. So long again!"

He jerked the door open; a long sighing draught ran through the cabin, and before him lay a blinding mist of flying snow. Those within could see, now, that the entire ravine was cloaked with shining white.

Into that whiteness stepped Shawn, and closed the door heavily behind him; a long silence held the people in the cabin.

"I didn't speak, Kitty," said Jim Berry, "because it didn't seem any use. If I told him that I meant nothing to you, what difference would it have made? He only would of laughed at me. But, my God, how I wish that you could forgive the harm that I've done you with him!"

She merely shrugged her shoulders.

And then old Shannon went to her, took her by the arm, and led her to the door. He raised his head, and the lips which had not spoken a human word for those many long months now said in a strangely hollow voice:

"Child, you love him. Go after him and bring him back. Or go after him and follow him where he rides."

Thomas and Berry, their hair fairly lifting on their heads, raised themselves on their elbows and stared in mortal wonder; and Kitty Bowen looked up to the hermit as if to a ghost.

"Do you understand?" repeated Shannon. "Go after him; fall on your knees in front of him; beg him to take you back. Are you afraid? I'll take you to him!"

And he led her, stunned and unresisting, out of the house and into the open. A great whirl of wind, filled with snow particles, formed around them, and the cold gripped them with a numbing power. Still he strode straight forward, threw open the door of the horse shed, and entered, leading Kitty Bowen like a captive behind him.

There they saw Shawn in the act of drawing up the cinches of his horse.

"Go to him now," said the hermit. "Fall on your knees. Tell him that you have been a light woman, but not a wicked one!"

The outlaw, more agape at Shannon than

at the girl, stood back from his mustang; Kitty, like one hypnotized, did exactly as Shannon had directed. She fell on her knees before Terry Shawn.

"Oh Terry, Terry!" said the girl. "I've been a silly fool, but I didn't mean harm. Will you forgive me? Will you take me back?"

Terry Shawn caught her from the floor and held her close in his arms; he had no time to speak a word, for Shannon's voice broke heavily in on them again.

"Go back to the house, child. Take your coat because you'll need all the warmth you can get. Come back here quickly. You must start away at once!"

She went, never dreaming of disobeying, but as she hurried through the door of the shed, Shawn protested: "It's not right to drive a girl like that into this sort of weather."

"This is her last chance to get away," he replied. "Otherwise she'll he frozen in with the rest."

"Isn't that better, Mr. Shannon?"

"Left with an old man who couldn't protect her, and those two?"

"Man, man," said Shawn, "they'd never harm a girl!"

311

"They're worse than they themselves guess," answered the hermit.

"Then I'll stay here with them."

"And be trapped! I know the sheriff of this county, and if he rides slowly on a trail, he rides forever. Boy, I have broken a great vow for your sake today; don't let me break it in vain. Do as I tell you to do, and begin by saddling Sky Pilot."

"Are you riding with us?"

"I am riding with you to show you some short cuts through the lower ravines, so that you can get out of the danger of a snow blockade. But I don't ride Sky Pilot. Put your own saddle on him."

"Hold on—" cried Shawn.

"He is your horse," said the hermit. "I give my part in him freely to you, and no man has a greater right to him than I have. He is yours!"

40

YOU WHO LOVE diamonds, suppose that the greatest of all diamonds were put in your hands? Still it was nothing compared with the joy that filled the heart of Terence Shawn as he heard this speech. But he was sobered instantly, and exclaimed, "I never could ride him!"

"Get into the saddle while I hold his head," said the hermit, "and he will never trouble you; he will be a good servant to you the rest of your life."

"He is like a child to you," said Terry Shawn. "How can you give him away?"

"Like should go to like," said the old man, his face touched with pain which he instantly banished. "What is he to me except a plaything? To you, he's the other half of a soul!"

"Partner," said Terry Shawn slowly, "you're a fine man, God knows; but if I let you do this, I'm a snake. I thought that you knew me, but you don't. I thought that you figgered me for what I am, but I see that you think I'm some honest puncher or farmer, maybe. Lemme tell you the truth. If you never heard of Terence Shawn before, I'll tell you what he is: he's a robber, a waster, a no-good gent. And I can't take no more from you than I've taken already!"

The hermit smiled.

"Those two inside my house," he said, pointing, "are much worse than they think. They have not been outlawed, and therefore they still think that they are worthy of living like honest men. You, my friend, have been outlawed, and you despise yourself because a sentence has been passed on you. Yet you are better than you think."

"Ten states would like to have the hanging of me," admitted Shawn gravely.

"A wise man," said the other, "once said that there are only two great sins—cruelty and cowardice. You never have been cruel, my young friend, and you never have been cowardly. If you have fought, it has been the fighting of tiger with tiger; you have not taken advantage of helpless men. You are better than you dream, Terence Shawn, and for the sake of this girl you can settle down to a useful, steady life."

"Who are you?" said the outlaw, filled with wonder and awe. "God knows I hope that what you say about me may be right. Whether right or not, I'm going to give it a chance. But who are you? What brought you here?"

"Sin," said the hermit gravely. "Terrible, mortal sin brought me here, sin for which no repentance is complete enough. Silence and misery and cold and pain are not enough!"

The outlaw listened, struck dumb. To attempt to persuade or comfort this man never occurred to him, any more than it would have occurred to attempt to persuade Mount Shannon's granite cliffs and grinning cañons. His own affairs seemed suddenly shrunk to a small scale; his own troubles were as nothing; and such matters as wind and weather were not to be regarded.

Kitty Bowen came hurrying back, bundled with wraps to face the long ride. For himself, the hermit flung over his shoulders a ragged sheepskin cloak of home manufacture, and gave another to Shawn. So they emerged from the shed with the three horses, and the white world lay before them.

"Which way do you wish to ride?" asked the hermit.

"North, north!" said Terry Shawn eagerly. "Out of this range as fast as I can go. But first I'm taking Kitty home!"

"I'd never go," said the girl. "Terry, what are you asking of me?"

And her eyes grew big with tears.

"D'you think that I'd ride you over the mountains in weather like this?" asked Terry Shawn. "Back you go and—"

"Young man, young man," said the her-

315

mit, "opportunity comes only once. Now God has given her to you, take her and keep her. You will find a minister in the first small village, no doubt. Be married there; ride on; your home is where you two are found together; and before long, you'll find a way of settling peacefully. From the moment you have her, my friend, you never will be tempted to any crime.

"Listen to him!" said the girl. "Oh, Terry, I think that we can believe him!"

"He's the law and the gospel to me," answered the boy solemnly. "What he says, I'll do. Sir, would you lead the way?"

"I'll hold Sky Pilot while you mount him. Are you ready?"

"I'm ready. He'll leave me at the sky, though!"

"Watch, then!"

Standing at the head of the stallion, Shannon soothed it with a word and laid his hand on the reins, but Sky Pilot showed not the slightest concern when Shawn approached and put his foot in the stirrup, and when the latter swung into the saddle, the stallion merely shook himself a little and then pricked cheerful ears.

"By the lord," breathed Terry Shawn, "I think you're right. He's not goin' to pitch. What in the world did you do to him?"

"You did it yourself yesterday," said the other.

"I only got him so that he would let me walk beside him," protested the outlaw.

"Ay," nodded the hermit, "but in this world, what no longer fears us already has begun to love us or despise us, and not even Sky Pilot could despise you, my friend!"

With this explanation Shawn had to rest content; indeed; he had little chance to think, during the next few moments, for Sky Pilot, if not viciously determined to dismount his new rider, was at least so filled with high spirits that he could not and would not keep still. Up on his hind legs he reared suddenly and beat at the air with his armed hoofs, then wheeled and plunged away, frolicking and lashing out with his heels. Twice he skidded on snow-covered rocks on which his shoes rang loudly; back and forth across the ravine he raced and played like a lamb in spring a twelve-hundred-pound lamb with muscles of steel.

As suddenly as he began this nonsense, he dropped it and went calmly along beside the others.

"It's like sitting on the back of a bird," said Shawn, in a voice trembling with excitement.

"Or a thunderbolt," said the girl. "Didn't he nearly put you down a dozen times?"

"Never once! He looked wild, didn't he? I tell you he softened everything. Once I lost a stirrup, and he was dog-trotting in a minute. I tell you, he's human, he's better than human—I never knew a man that was worthy of brushing his coat!"

"It is true," said Shannon. "He has learned how to hate and he has learned how to love while he is still young. My young friend, he should go on to great things, with you to ride him!"

"I'll only keep him," said Shawn sincerely, "so long as I have to ride hard to break away from this section of the range where I'm known; but when I manage to settle down to a straight life with Kitty, I'll send him back to you—"

"Is he meant," said the hermit with a smile, "to carry an old man through a solitary forest or to give some pleasure to the eyes of ten thousand people?"

It was reasoning well over the head of Terry Shawn.

"If you have a beautiful daughter some

day," said the hermit, "will you want to send her away to the woods to marry a recluse, or keep her in the world where everyone may enjoy her beauty? Ah, lad, the setting is as important as the jewel, even if it doesn't cost as much. Take Sky Pilot. God bring you luck with him. When I came back and saw that you'd mastered him, I knew that he should belong to you. Now say no more about it. Here's where the road forks for us. We can take either of the two ravines. That on the left would be dangerous going, but there's not apt to be any observers along the way. This on the right is easier and quicker, but it might have other riders coming up—"

"We'll chance it," answered Shawn. "You think that the sheriff here rides in all weathers. Well, he does, but he can't get posses to follow him through a storm like this!"

"The storm has fallen away," said Shannon. "And that sheriff will always do more than you expect. Ride on, however. We'll take the right-hand ravine. Keep a little behind me; I'll go on first!"

So he broke trail for them, as it were, and the two drew together behind him. They spoke very little, but looked often and wonderingly on one another. And once he found that Kitty was crying silently and asked her what troubled her.

"Only that I hardly can stand it, Terry, to think that everything is going to turn out right for us!"

"Not yet! We're a long cry from that!"

"He said so—and he can't be wrong—he can't be wrong!"

Shawn himself felt the same superstitious conviction that the hermit spoke as an inspired man; content and surety filled him as they jogged down the trail, and now, rapidly, they passed into a new climate. For the storm, which had been dying down every moment during the past hour, had now fallen to the dimensions of an ordinary snowfall, and this, as they dropped lower and lower down the ravine, began to thin out.

Still they could look back and observe Mount Shannon wrapped, as it were, in thunder, but the southern sky momently grew brighter; they had come down to a warmer level, and their heavy wraps were almost too hot. A late spring of careless joy was rising in the hearts of the lovers; before them rode a guide and guard who was, they felt invincible; and behind them lay not only Mount Shannon but all the dangers and the follies and the mistakes of Shawn's past life. Like a region of shadows it appeared to him now.

They saw Shannon stop, throw out an arm, and then whirl his horse about. He came rapidly back to them.

"Here!" said Shannon. "We'll ride straight down that cañon. They're coming straight up to us—I was right—the sheriff and twenty men, I think, and every one of them is mounted on a fresh horse. Ride fast! God bring us one more touch of snow to cover our tracks!"

That prayer was instantly answered by the passing of a whirlpool of wind, heavily laden with snow, and as the whirlwind dispersed, the floor of the ravine was loaded with fresh inches of snow.

41

SWIFTLY THEY WENT down the little cañon which opened off the course of the main ravine, and, doubling to the right, they came upon a second valley, broader and leading well on in the direction which they were following.

"It is all the better," said Shannon, whose

cheerfulness was growing with every moment; "we have better going here and—"

"On the right!" snapped Shawn. "They're coming. Ride, Kitty—Shannon, ride for it!"

They swung their horses about and got them into a gallop just before a mass of riders burst out of the low woods ahead of them. How it had happened so quickly they could not imagine, unless it was that the sheriff, catching a glimpse of his enemy in the first ravine and seeing them disappear, had guessed that they would try this second passage. At any rate, there was the familiar gawky figure of the sheriff riding with all his customary skill and boldness.

Behind him came the pick of the county and the range, as was proved by the first volley that they poured into the fugitives from long range, for the very first round of shots knocked the hat from Shannon's head and slashed the girl's horse across the hip—not a serious wound but one that made the animal begin to pitch wildly, so that Kitty was well-nigh thrown to the ground.

Shawn turned in the saddle and began to drop shots around the pursuers. He put them close to the ears of the sheriff; he kicked up the snow in white puffs before the reaching feet of the horses, but not a man faltered, and not a man fell out of the race; they were riding today to make a kill, and that was apparent.

Shawn took stock of the horses on which they three were mounted. Kitty was a feather-weight, and her nag would hold up; Sky Pilot, of course, could laugh at the whole world, and that left Shannon. There was the weak point. He was no light burden in the saddle, and his horse could not stretch out with such an impost. Cutting down their speed to keep with him, they were letting the posse climb up on their tracks slowly and surely. A worried glance from Kitty showed that she understood perfectly, but still Shannon was smiling and calm.

He shouted to his younger companion, "Keep a strong heart, my lad. I have an assurance that all will be well!"

No sooner had he spoken than a violent blow in the side made Shawn sway in the saddle, and a bitter pain slipped over his ribs, and the hot blood ran freely down. There was no hiding it. Even the men in the rear had seen the swaying of the rider for there was a yell of exultation from them.

There was no concealing that wound—from Kitty, least of all. And she pulled her horse over beside Shawn and watched him with a white face.

"We have to surrender, Terry!" she said.

"Never," he answered through his teeth. "Terry, we're lost, we're lost! Only trust to the sheriff—"

He waved to her, as though to signify that he would not waste his strength in argument, and then, turning a little in the saddle, he looked back with a sort of leonine fierceness upon the rout behind him.

"This way—to the right!" called Shannon suddenly.

They swerved into the mouth of a shallow valley, and, riding at full speed, they gained enough to have a full bend of the ravine between them and the pursuit. Here Shannon reined close to Shawn and looked into the narrowing eyes of the youth and the gray, set face.

"Pull into those trees!" he commanded. "Dress that wound; and stay there till I come back. I'm going to play a game with this posse."

"We'll stay together—" began Shawn, when the other cut him short with an imperious air of command. "Do as I say. Into that cover with both of you!"

And like children they obeyed, and swung aside into the thicket. Shannon went straight ahead, and so did the echoes multiply the sounds of his running horse, even to the two behind him, it seemed that several riders must be pressing up the valley.

They were not well in shelter before the posse came by them, the men leaning forward to the pace, the horses shining with sweat, their ears laid back to their work, and their snaky heads stretched forth. First came the tall sheriff; behind him was the main body; a few hundred yards to the rear a little clump of stragglers. They saw this, then Terry tore off coat and shirt, and the girl saw a long raw furrow in his side, scraping across the bones of the ribs. There was no danger from it; it was painful but never could kill except through the loss of blood, and between them they had skill enough to manage a worse hurt than this.

If only Shannon could keep the posse employed—if only he could draw them sufficiently away!

He had gone straight on down the valley until it began to dwindle and the floor rose sharply. Mercilessly he drove his horse, and yet for all his driving he could not gain ground on the head of the pursuit, for there rode the sheriff and the best of his fighting men on chosen horses. They felt that their quarry was before them at last, and they were sparing neither whip nor spur.

The ground rose, now, to a low divide—a narrow pass littered with boulders, and here Shannon dismounted.

Before him there was the beginning of another ravine, rapidly deepening as it progressed—a little valley with a rocky floor where the tracks even of galloping horses hardly would appear. There he might have ridden and striven to hide himself in some nook of the broken walls. Instead, he chose to dismount, and, letting his horse gallop away, he took place behind a great rock, and when the sheriff came in sight with the utmost care he placed a bullet mere inches from the cheek of Lank Heney. Another ball, a nearer thing than he had expected, clipped a horse on the shoulder.

The whole posse split like rain on a roof. Some poured to one side and some to another. Many dismounted; he heard a clamoring of voices, and presently he had glimpses of men struggling up through the boulders to take him on the flanks.

He was not fighting; he was only pretending to fight; but all the skill which he had learned in hunting on the broad breast of Mount Shannon was brought into play, now. Wherever an enemy fairly showed himself, a bullet was sure to sing past close to his head, and the posse began to advance more slowly, more cautiously, though the voice of the sheriff could clearly be heard urging them on.

Down the farther ravine the clattering hoofs of the riderless horse beat up the echoes, and the sheriff was crying:

"There's only one of them here holding us back! Press on, boys! We're losing miles and miles—we're losing the whole game, and we had 'em in our hands!"

Twice he himself showed head and shoulders, as he climbed recklessly to the front, and twice he ducked as bullets whisked past him. And so, shifting restlessly from rock to rock, his rifle growing hot in his hands, old Shannon kept the posse at bay for a round twenty minutes of priceless time. His own horse was long out of sight, and he felt that his work had been accomplished.

His position had grown mortally dangerous, in the meantime. On the right the sheriff had pushed up into a flanking position;

and on the left two others were able to rake him. Twice leaden slugs splashed on the face of a rock nearby; then a hammer blow struck Shannon on the side of the head, and he rolled helplessly on his back.

There Lank Heney found him, eyes rapidly glazing, arms thrown wide. He leaned over the fallen man, then he kneeled by his side.

"It's Shannon!" he exclaimed. "Man, man, how'd you happen to get mixed up in this game?"

But the hermit had fallen back into his familiar role. He only raised himself a little on one elbow and pointed down the shallow valley before them with a smile of triumph, as though to indicate that he was satisfied with the work he had done in placing his two companions beyond the reach of the law. The he fell back, one struggle convulsed him, his eyes closed.

"Ride on like hell down the far valley!" shouted the sheriff to his men. "We've still got a ghost of a show!"

But he kept at the side of the fallen man, waiting for the last moment, full of awe and wonder such as comes on the sternest when a man lays down his life for a friend.

The closed eyes opened; a flash of life

appeared in them, but they were looking far off beyond the face of Lank Heney.

"Death is not the worst evil, my dear!" said Shannon, and with that his eyes opened still wider, grew fixed, and the final tremor passed through his body.

Epilogue

SHERIFF LANK HENEY, as a man who never forgot, wrote down all that episode in red in his heart of hearts, more so since the mystery never was explained. The mysterious Shannon died, died with words upon his lips, but thereafter nothing whatever was learned about his past. The dashing young outlaw, Shawn, never was heard of again, and many felt that he must have lost his footing, in going along one of the narrow, snow-covered mountain trails, and been ground to nothing on the rocky floor of some canon half a mile below. Neither did the girl return, and for her Mr. Bowen made a brief but terrible appeal to all his fellow citizens of the range. However, at the end of a few days, he sent out word that he was convinced that further search was useless; this matter was in the hands of God; it was folly for him to attempt to alter the ways of divinity.

What brought the matter all again into the mind of the good sheriff was that, when hunting a slippery cattle thief through those same highlands at the knees of Mount Shannon, he came to the spot where Shannon had died and where they had given him shallow sepulture among the boulders.

He found the spot; but the heap of stones was vastly greater than the one which he and his men had made, and a big block of gray granite had been hewn roughly and with great, deeply bitten letters. The sheriff read the legend with attention:

"Here lies Shannon, the bravest, the gentlest, and the best of all partners. God give him the happiness that he gave to his friends!"

Now when the sheriff read this notice, he bit his lip and narrowed his eyes, for a keen thought smote him like a pain and never left him thereafter.

However, it was four years after this that he was riding far north and came to a little-frequented corner of the range, for the vast mountains and the broken trails made the district difficult of access. And when he twisted his way through this region of cliffs and rough valleys, he came suddenly on a little paradise in the midst of the wilderness—four-mile ravine, a quarter as wide as it was long, the floor covered with the richest of river detritus, and all that sweep of land skillfully put to use.

He saw it from above and marked the order of the place with a cheerful eye; then, having passed down the trail, he rode through sweet-smelling orchards, and fields of springing grain, and wide, rich pastures, where blood horses walked and fine cattle wandered. All that the heart could wish for was being raised on that ground, so it appeared to the sheriff. He took smiling heed of it, and so he came to the house.

It was not overly large, but vastly comfortable. It stood near the bank of the creek, surrounded by a vast tangle of garden which was allowed to run half wild. Farther up the stream was the mill and the mill dam, and around the mill there appeared to be a tiny village; at least, the signs of a carpenter, miller, blacksmith, storekeeper, and half a dozen others were exposed here, and a crossroads seemed to indicate that people came down from some distance in the mountains to make their trading headquarters here.

The sheriff regarded these matters with the greatest pleasure, for it is always a delightful thing to see prosperity; particularly on what seemed to him such a princely scale! And then he took note of three handsome youngsters tumbling in the garden; and beyond the garden a bit of fine pasture with a beautiful chestnut stallion standing in it . . .

It was the sight of the stallion which gave him his clue, after all. He rode closer. He stared with hungry eyes. There was no doubt about it; it was Sky Pilot.

Then he turned sharply and regarded the children. At last he called to the oldest, a sweet-faced girl of seven, and when she came running, he lifted her up beside him in the saddle.

"Now, honey," said he, "I want you to tell me something. You got a fine mother and daddy, I take it."

She nodded; she was not attracted by the manner of Lank Heney.

"You remember this. Say it to your mother and your daddy the first minute that you can find 'em: 'Sheriff Heney has been here, and he wishes you well.' D'you hear?"

"Yes."

"Repeat it now."

She obeyed.

"Ay," said Lank Heney, "you got the very look of her. And before you're grown, honey, you'll be at work breakin' hearts!"

With that, he rode slowly down the trail beside the creek, and the little girl scampered into the house, out of which presently a man ran, saddle and bridle in hand. He called the stallion, and Sky Pilot came to him like a blast of stormwind, vaulting the fence. However, with the horse beside him, the man hesitated, and looking long and earnestly after the other, as Heney disappeared down the road, at last, he seemed to feel that it was best to let the other go unhailed and unvisited.

He turned thoughtfully back into the house, the door closed softly behind him, and all was as it had been before. But not quite. For a great shadow had been lifted from that happy valley on this day, never to return.